Out in the square, Louise was backing along the short path in front of her house, trying to get the dispute off the street and indoors where it belonged. But Lydia Harris, Pat's mother, wanted it out in the open.

'It's as much your responsibility as his!' she yelled. 'He's your flamin' son! All you're doin' is shieldin' him!'

'I'm doin' sod all of the sort!' Louise retorted. 'Now you come in here an' we can talk this over like grown-up women, instead of slangin' each other out here like brawlin' kids.'

'Oh, it's embarrassin' you, is it?' Lydia folded her arms and looked up and down the Square. 'I suppose you don't want your neighbours knowin' about it.'

By the same author

The Outsider
The Dark Side of the Sun

EastEnders

Home Fires Burning
Good Intentions
The Flower of Albert Square
Blind Spots
Hopes and Horizons

HUGH MILLER

Swings and Roundabouts

EastEnders – Book 2

By arrangement with the
British Broadcasting Corporation

GRAFTON BOOKS

A Division of the Collins Publishing Group

LONDON GLASGOW
TORONTO SYDNEY AUCKLAND

Grafton Books
A Division of the Collins Publishing Group
8 Grafton Street, London W1X 3LA

Published by Grafton Books 1985
Reprinted 1986

EastEnders copyright © BBC 1985
This novel copyright © Hugh Miller, Julia Smith
and Tony Holland 1985

ISBN 0-586-06810-4

Printed and bound in Great Britain by
Collins, Glasgow

Set in Times

For Anna Wing

Prologue
1957

Harold Legg put his stethoscope in his case and moved away from the bed. At the door he paused and looked across at Albert Beale. He was gaunt and pale, so thin now that his head scarcely dented the pillow.

'I'll pop back and see you later.'

Albert nodded, unable to speak. His mouth gulped the air as if he were drinking.

Louise was waiting in the room below, restlessly twisting her finger rings. As the doctor came down the stairs she watched his face carefully, trying to read what he might not say.

'He's calmer now, Lou.'

'Thank God for that. He really gave me a turn.'

Harold took out his prescription pad, scribbled something on the top sheet and tore it off. 'This should help. A little.' He put down the slip and looked squarely at Louise. 'He's very weak, because his lungs aren't passing on the proper support to his muscles.' That was the gentle way of putting it. Among themselves, doctors called someone in Albert's condition a respiratory cripple. 'The best we can do, really, is see that he rests and gets oxygen whenever he needs it.'

'It didn't seem to do him no good this mornin'.' Louise's reproach was aimed at the oxygen rather than the doctor. 'You'd think there'd be somethin' that'd let him get a decent breath.'

Harold sighed. There was less room for reassurance as each day passed. Albert's emphysema had reached a point where there was practically no elasticity remaining in his lungs.

'The medicine will make him drowsy. He won't feel so panicky after a while.'

Lou picked up the prescription and folded it. 'I'll go round the chemist's after the kids have had their dinner.'

'There's something on there for you, too.'

'Me?'

'Yes. I don't think you realize how run-down you are. When did you last have a full night's sleep?'

Louise shrugged. She had no wish to be the focus of his professional attention. 'There's nothin' wrong with me. I'm a bit tired, maybe, but that's all.'

'A bit tired now, but physically exhausted before you know it. You must try to get a break during the day, to make up for what you lose at night.' He pointed at the prescription. 'It's a tonic. Make sure you take it regularly, until it's all used up.'

He watched the reluctant nod, remembering her as she had been during the forties, when he first met her. Like her husband upstairs, Louise no longer bore a trace of youth. She was forty-two but looked fifty. In time, probably, she would begin to look better. Albert wouldn't.

'Like a cuppa, would you?'

Harold shook his head. 'I've a clinic to get through after my rounds.' He glanced at his watch. 'It's ten past eleven now. I'll be finished by about three. I'll come back and have a look at him then.'

As he went out to the hall Louise followed him. 'He's not been this bad before, has he?' she said.

'No, not quite as bad.' He opened the door.

'It's more than a week now, an' all he's got is worse.' Louise was deducing aloud, moving towards a grim conclusion. She looked at Harold, waiting for him to voice it. But he didn't.

'I'll have that cuppa when I come round this afternoon,' he said. He was off and out past the gate before Louise could say any more. She watched his tall figure stride

8

across Albert Square to the corner by his surgery, where his car was parked. He waved to her as he got in.

Louise closed the door, went through to the kitchen and put on the kettle. She was determined not to entertain the dark thought that had descended on her a minute ago. She didn't want to start wondering, either, why Dr Legg was going to visit Albert a second time that day. Instead of brooding, she worked out her timetable.

First, she would take a cup of tea up to Albert and sit with him while she drank her own. After that she would come down and get dinner ready for the twins, Pauline and Pete, who usually got home from school about ten past twelve. When they went back at ten to one, she would start the weekly wash. By the time that was done and she'd tackled some dusting, the doctor would be back.

It always made Louise feel better to plan the hours ahead. It was terrible when she had to find things to do; she was used to having her time spoken for. Nowadays, there was always the danger of arriving at a loose end, yet it didn't seem so long ago that she couldn't move for her kids and their demands.

'Them days are gone, girl,' she murmured, getting down the tea caddy.

The young ones were leaving the nest, as Albert was forever saying to her. It was sadly true, and at odd times of the day Louise found the house uncomfortably quiet.

'To think you used to kick up a stink about their noise,' her friend Ethel had said, when Louise complained to her about the daily hours of silence. 'You often said you'd be glad when they was all up in years and out on their own, remember?'

Louise remembered. She was certainly getting that wish, with no allowance for second thoughts. Harry, the oldest son, worked in a hotel in Brighton; they only saw him once a month. Dora still lived at home, but she worked all day at the hairdresser's and went out most nights with her boyfriend, so she wasn't often about the house. Kenneth had ten months of his National Service to finish, and for the past year Ronnie had been out all day, Monday to Saturday, running the fruit and vegetable stall now that his father was too ill to cope with it. Most evenings he would come in, get washed, change his clothes and go out again with his mates. Even the twins weren't the eternal noisy presence they used to be.

When she took the tea up to the bedroom Albert looked as if he was asleep, but as she tiptoed closer his eyes opened.

'Feel up to a drink do you, love?'

He nodded. Louise put down the cups and leaned across the bed, grasping his shoulders and raising him. It was like lifting a child, she thought. She slid the pillows from her side of the bed on top of his and eased him gently on to them.

'There.'

She held the cup in front of him until he had closed the fingers of both hands around it. He panted softly as he stared at the cup, waiting for the rhythm of his breathing to slow before he attempted to drink.

'I've got a chit for some new medicine. We'll see how you get along with that, eh?'

Albert's eyes turned to her, wide and anxious looking, as they always were when he had one of his bad spells. He made a little smile, deepening the lines on his cheeks. 'Feel a bit better, last couple of minutes,' he wheezed. ''Bout time, too.'

'The rest's doin' you good, just like you was told it would. Now drink that up, it'll do you a bit of good an' all.'

She sipped her own tea, thinking of how gradual it had been, Albert's decline from delicate health to the condition of an invalid. For a time during the war he had been a prisoner of the Japanese. That was when the real vigour had been driven out of him; his resilience had

10

been destroyed by cruelty, starvation and disease. For five years until 1951, when he turned forty, he had managed to run the market stall full time. But his lungs had been getting progressively worse. Every winter he suffered at least two attacks of bronchitis; afterwards he was always a little weaker, a shade less capable of being on his feet all day in every kind of weather.

'Fancy a boiled egg for dinner, smashed up in a cup with butter?'

Albert shook his head.

'You've got to eat, love.' She nodded at the oxygen cylinder by the bed. 'You can't live on the stuff that comes out of there.'

'I couldn't hold down an egg, Lou.' His voice was reedy, like a frail old man's. 'Maybe tonight.'

When he had taken less than half the tea he handed the cup back to Louise. She settled him down again, tucked in the covers and kissed his forehead.

'I don't doubt young Pete'll be up botherin' you as soon as he gets in. Better get all the rest you can in the meantime.'

The twins came racketing in through the back door just after five past twelve. They were both red-faced from running.

'I won!' Pauline yelled, throwing herself on to a chair. Her fair hair was plastered to her forehead. 'You owe me a tanner!'

'I was in first,' her stocky brother complained.

'That wasn't the rules. It was first in and *sittin' down* was the winner.'

'Cheat!'

'Mum, tell him he owes me a tanner.'

Louise was still busy with the frying pan. She glanced over her shoulder. 'Fight it out between yourselves. An' quietly. Your dad's tryin' to sleep.'

'Can I go up an' see him?' Pete asked. Of all the

children, he was the one most strongly attached to his father. 'I'll be quiet.'

'Go on, then. But don't stop long. He's to get all the peace an' quiet he can.'

As Pete left the kitchen Pauline stood up and crossed to her mother's side. 'Listen, Mum,' she whispered, suppressing a giggle, 'guess what somebody's wrote on the wall of the girls' lavs at school?'

'Nothin' rude, I hope. If it is, I don't want to hear it.'

'No, it ain't rude. It's chalked up in real big letters – Kathy Hills loves Pete Beale.'

Louise rolled her eyes. Twelve years old and already her son was somebody's heart throb. 'Who put it there?'

'Kathy Hills herself. One of the girls saw her. Mary Birch says Kathy's real serious about our Pete.'

Louise sniffed. 'You'd better not take that tanner off him, then. He'll likely be savin' up for an engagement ring.'

There was a sudden clattering as Pete came running back down the stairs. 'Mum!'

Louise dropped the frying pan on to the cooker and ran through the front room. Pete practically collided with her.

'What is it?'

'Dad! It's Dad – he's chokin'!'

Louise pushed past him and hurried up the stairs. Pete turned frightened eyes on his sister as she came through. 'He looks bad, Pauline. Terrible.'

Ever practical, Pauline strode out to the hall. 'I'll get the doctor,' she called.

Pete went back upstairs. He found Louise supporting Albert on one arm, holding his shoulders up off the bed as he struggled to pull in air. With her free hand she was trying to operate the oxygen tap.

'Quick,' she snapped at Pete. 'Get this turned on and put the mask over his face.'

Pete had never used the equipment before. He began

12

fumbling with the tap and untangling the mask from the cylinder at the same time.

'Come on, Pete.'

Albert's mouth was blue. The noise in his throat was like the frantic rustling of paper.

'Hurry up!'

Louise shifted Albert, trying to find a position where the weakened chest muscles could work better. She looked up as the cylinder gurgled and oxygen began escaping along the line.

'That's it. Now just hold the thing on his face.'

Albert sagged as Pete tried to put the mask in position. The noise in his throat dropped to a hiss.

'Mum . . .' Pete looked at his mother. He was scared.

She was staring at Albert, rocking him. 'Come on, love. Come on . . .'

She began shaking him as his eyelids lowered and his jaw dropped open. A thin line of saliva trailed from the side of his mouth.

'Albert!'

For an instant his eyes opened again and he was looking at her, staring straight into her, then she felt him soften and his head dropped forward.

'Albert! Don't!'

Dazed suddenly, her mind recoiling from a certainty she wouldn't face, Louise allowed herself to be taken aside by Pauline. Dr Legg stepped forward. He had run all the way from his surgery. Swiftly he unrolled an instrument pack on to the bed covers.

'Take your mum downstairs,' he murmured to Pauline as he fitted a needle to a syringe. 'You go too, Pete.'

They waited in the kitchen, saying nothing, not looking at each other. After several minutes Harold Legg came down. He told Pauline to put on the kettle and make some tea, then he led Louise through to the couch in the front room, guiding her with an arm on her shoulder.

'Sit down, Lou.'

She obeyed like a child. Harold took her hand in both of his.

'It's over. Albert's got some peace, now.'

'But he was feeling better,' she complained, fighting the truth. 'He said so, not an hour since.'

'Lou, listen. If it hadn't happened today, it would certainly have happened tomorrow.'

She shook her head. 'He's only forty-six . . .'

'He was terribly ill. But that's over for him now. Try to think of him not being in pain any more, not having to fight for every mouthful of air.'

All at once Louise felt the same way she did long years before, when she had finally confronted the fact that Albert was missing somewhere on the other side of the world. Now, as then, she felt the cold, creeping tendrils of loss. This time, there were no elements of doubt or hope. The certainty was dark and total. Albert would never come back.

She looked up at the doctor. 'He didn't want to go,' she whispered.

In the kitchen, Pete began to cry against his sister's shoulder.

1

'There comes a time,' Dr Roger Lewis said, 'when you have to ask yourself if you're really getting anywhere in general practice, or if you're just pissing against the wind.'

Harold Legg smiled at him. 'Is that really what happened? Or did the new job come up and you jumped at it, then worked out your excuse after the event?'

It was a bright Saturday morning at the end of March, 1964. They were sitting at opposite sides of the desk in Harold's basement surgery, drinking coffee. It was Easter. Roger had sat in the waiting room for twenty minutes while Harold attended to three patients with urgent complaints. Now, they were taking a quick refreshment before leaving to spend the weekend at Roger's holiday cottage in Eastbourne.

'I mean it,' Roger said defensively. 'I was getting in a rut. Three months ago I looked at myself in the shaving mirror and saw middle-age gazing back at me.'

'Oh come on now, Roger . . .' He was forty-three, a year older than Harold, a bachelor who took great care over his appearance. With his shock of black hair and healthy pink features he looked closer to thirty-five. 'Neither of us is into the declining years quite yet.'

'Galloping decline's built into a GP's job. I could feel myself getting older and more rancid every day.' Roger drained his cup and slapped it down on the saucer. 'For eleven years I've been toiling in that bloody practice, doling out drugs, forgetting what medicine's all about – reaching for my ballpoint instead of my stethoscope every time a patient walks in.'

'So, what you're saying is, you got fed up.'

'Right.'

'And you won't get fed up in Charlotte Street, treating hypochondria instead of illness?'

'That's a very simplistic view of private practice, Harold.'

'I just threw it in to balance your picture of general practice.'

They grinned at each other. Since their student days at Bart's, they had enjoyed the kind of friendship where mutual criticism and occasional slanging were perfectly in order.

'I'm pleased for you,' Harold said. 'You did well to get a partnership with Gilmour. He's well thought of. I always had the feeling it was just a matter of time before you went into the pinstripe-and-morning-coat branch of the trade, anyway.'

'You should be doing the same.'

Harold raised his bushy eyebrows. 'Me? That's ridiculous. Laughable.'

'You're throwing away your talent,' Roger insisted. 'And I'm not the only one who thinks that. If you moved up West you'd find yourself being offered some real challenges.'

'I get plenty here.'

'Listen. That paper you published in the BMJ – the one about the interpretation of electro-cardiograms – it was a knockout. Terribly erudite stuff. A lot of people were surprised when I told them the author was practising out of a rabbit-hole in Walford.'

Harold finished his coffee and stood up. 'This is where I belong, Roger. I'm helping the kind of people I want to help.'

'You're a romantic. There's a whole world of sophisticated medical practice out there – a world full of men and women with insight and flair. You belong among them.'

Harold shook his head. 'When I get a yen for the more

sophisticated stuff I spend a few of my free days working with my father.' Harold's father was a Consultant Cardiologist with hospital appointments as well as a private practice. 'You're the climbing type, Roger. I'm not. So we're both doing just fine.'

Roger groaned as he got out of the chair. 'You're a dead-ringer for Dr Kildare.'

'No.' Harold picked up his weekend bag from beside the desk. 'I'm not that idealistic. Not half so pretty, either.'

They went out through the waiting room. As Harold locked up Roger climbed the steps to street level and stood looking across Albert Square.

'This place has hardly changed since the war,' he said. He had visited the surgery and the house above it several times over the years. The first time he had been to the house was the day when Harold was married. They had both been students at the time. It seemed ages ago.

'Outwardly it hasn't changed much,' Harold said, coming up the steps. He stood looking up at the house, which was divided into flats now. 'Sometimes, you know, I get the eerie feeling I've slipped back in time. I almost expect to see Judith twitch the curtain aside and wave to me.'

Harold had been a widower for twenty years. They had been married only a few months when a dormant bomb exploded in the ground behind the house. Judith had been in the garden at the time; she was killed by flying masonry.

'Odd, isn't it?' He turned to Roger, who was smiling rather sadly. 'I only knew her two years in all, yet my memory of her is as vivid as ever.'

As they walked to Roger's car – it was more reliable on long trips than Harold's old Wolseley – a young woman across the way waved to Harold. He waved back.

'Pretty girl,' Roger remarked.

17

'Very pretty. Pauline Beale. I brought her and her twin brother into the world.'

Before they had reached the car two more people had greeted Harold.

'I can see part of the attraction of working here,' Roger said. 'The people transmit a lot of their warmth, don't they?'

'You said much the same thing the day Judith and I got married,' Harold reminded him. 'An East End practice would suit you, too, if you weren't such an incurable social climber.'

The Queen Victoria was a public house on the corner of Albert Square and Bridge Street. That morning the air inside was thick with smoke and the noise of Saturday drinkers, bawling to make themselves heard as they gossiped, swopped jokes, made pronouncements on the state of British football and paused, occasionally, to gulp down their pints of Luxford and Copley's Bitter.

Alf Barrett, the landlord, paused between serving customers to exchange views with Ethel Skinner, who had entrenched herself in the angle between the counter and the partition separating the two bars. Their conversation had been going on in instalments for nearly ten minutes.

'In my view,' Alf said, thoughtfully scratching one feathery sideburn, 'things'd be better all round if folks would just live an' let live.'

'That's all right as far as it goes.' Ethel nodded at the topic of their exchange, a pair of West Indian youths at the end of the bar. 'But we're not livin' as we want, are we? We're not bein' *let* live our own way. They're swarmin' all over the place nowadays, changin' everythin', bendin' our customs to suit themselves.'

'Ah, well . . .' Alf's true opinion on anything controversial was never likely to get aired in the bar. A landlord couldn't afford to be taking sides. 'There's good an' bad in everythin', isn't there?'

'A lot more bad than good in them lot, if you ask me.' Ethel waggled her head disapprovingly as one of the coloured youths glanced her way. 'Folk ought to stay where they come from.'

'It's a point of view, Ethel,' Alf murmured, moving away. 'It's certainly a point of view.'

Ethel took a swallow from her glass and looked around for somebody else to talk to. Normally she would have her husband with her, but William was getting more Saturday work at the docks these days. Her friend Lou had said she might come in for a couple, but there was no sign of her.

She noticed that a tall, good-looking man by the door was staring at her and she turned away sharply, pretending there was something in her eye. A married woman, she always reminded herself firmly, couldn't go encouraging the attentions of strange, handsome men.

It would never have occurred to Ethel that the man's gaze was being held by her outlandish appearance. She wore a light brown suit with a purple belt that matched, almost, her purple rayon blouse with its big, flouncy bow at the neck. A brown beret was perched at a breezy angle atop her swatch of ginger curls. Her rouged cheeks and bright, oily lipstick were no less eccentric, nor were her ill-fitting dentures. People soon got used to Ethel's appearance, but at first sight she could be unnerving.

'Oh, there you are, Etty.' Louise pushed her way forward to the bar and propped herself on one elbow. 'What a flamin' mornin' I've had.'

'What's up now, then?'

Polly, the landlord's wife came forward and Louise asked for a bottle of Guinness. Ethel rummaged her purse out of her handbag and paid for it.

'It'd take less time to tell you what's not up,' Louise said. 'You know we've been plannin' an Easter Sunday dinner at my place, right? Me an' the kids, my three sisters an' their lot, my brother . . .'

19

'Yeah. You told me.'

'Well there I was, up to me hips in food an' drink, runnin' round like a blue-arsed fly makin' all the arrangements – an' now Queenie an' Alec have called off, our Dora says she wants to go to Clacton with her bloke, an' to top it all . . .' she paused to roll her eyes elaborately. 'To top it all, that daft sod of a brother of mine reckons he won't be able to get round until after five, 'cause he's helpin' out a mate at his stall on Club Row.'

Ethel pursed her carmine lips and shook her head in sympathy. 'As if you hadn't got enough on your plate, what with young Pete worryin' you rotten.'

'That's another thing.' Louise snatched up her glass and took a long swallow from it. When she put it down again there was the trace of a frothy moustache on her upper lip. 'He wants to bring that Pat Harris round to dinner tomorrow. The cheek of it.'

Ethel looked duly affronted. 'It isn't as if he don't know how you feel about her.'

'She put him up to it,' Louise said darkly. 'She's wormin' her way in – or she thinks she is.'

Two weeks earlier Pete had announced that he was planning to marry Pat, a girl he had known for only a few months. Since then his mother had argued with him, threatened him and even said she would never speak to him again if he went through with it. But he still seemed as determined as ever.

'Besotted with her, he is,' Louise grunted. 'Thinks the sun shines out of her bum.'

Ethel's face took on a knowing look. 'If a girl decides she's goin' to have a bloke, there's not a lot him nor anybody else can do to stop her.' Quite often in her not-quite forty-four years Ethel had seen herself in the role of temptress, although since her marriage at the age of twenty-five she had never thrust her allure at the opposite sex. 'Once men are hooked they lose their heads, Lou. Don't I know it.'

'He's not even a man yet, is he? Nineteen, that's all he is. God knows what his Dad would've said if he'd been alive to know it.'

Louise picked up her glass again. She was making further inroads on the Guinness when her second youngest son, Ronnie, appeared through the crowd around the door. He was wrapped in an old sheepskin coat and had a woollen cap pulled down over his ears.

'Hello, love,' Louise said as he came forward. 'Havin' a break?'

He nodded. 'Jackie off the jewellery stall's holdin' the fort for me.' He took a pound note from his pocket. 'Can I get you a drink? Ethel?'

Both women nodded. When Ronnie had ordered, Louise gave him the catastrophic news about the following day's dinner arrangements.

'That's a shame,' Ronnie said. The remark was as impassioned as any he ever made; since he was a child he had been very shy and never demonstrative. Louise had no recollection of him even losing his temper. His glass was halfway to his lips when he frowned and put it down again. 'Clacton? Did you say Dora's goin' to Clacton?'

'That's right,' Louise said. 'Got a lot of consideration, hasn't she?'

'She'd better not go there,' Ronnie said. 'Didn't you hear it on the news?'

'Hear what?'

'The Mods an' Rockers. They've been riotin' down there. They reckon it's that bad, the police can't handle it.'

'Oh my good God.' Louise looked stricken. 'She was plannin' to go there tonight. *Tonight*, soon as she finishes at the salon.'

'Somebody better stop her, then.'

Ethel was shaking her head again. 'I don't know what's up with the world.'

Louise gulped down her drink and snatched up her

handbag from the bar. 'I'll get round there right now an' tell her.' She frowned at Ronnie. 'Riotin', you say?'

He nodded. 'Hundreds of them. Smashin' up cafés an' hotels, wreckin' the arcades, beatin' up each other an' anybody that gets in their way.'

Louise turned to Ethel. 'I'll be seein' you, Et. Got to go an' get this sorted out.' She drew her coat about her and began pushing her way distractedly towards the door.

Ethel watched her friend go, thinking of all the times over the past few years when Louise's family had got her in a state like that. If it wasn't young Pete in trouble with the law, it was Harry rolling up at the house blind drunk and throwing up all over the new suite, or Dora keeping company with shady-looking men in big cars, or Kenny getting in fights.

'She's got a lot to put up with,' Ethel murmured, too quietly for Ronnie to hear. There were times when she was glad she hadn't any children of her own. Not many times, though.

2

Pete and Kenneth Beale were strolling together along Walford High Road. It had once been a regular Sunday morning ritual, as important in its way as going to church. They would walk round the borough in order to be seen, wearing the reputations they had spent all week justifying and enlarging. What had once been a conscious parading, however, was now only a means of passing time. They still had their reputations, but they mattered less each day as the community expanded and parochial values dwindled.

Kenneth, seven years older than Pete, was unquestionably a hard man. Nobody in his right mind got on the wrong side of Kenny Beale. He never looked for trouble, it was just that Kenny's reputation invited challengers. Even at twenty-six he still got involved in the odd rumble outside a pub, and he hadn't yet been beaten. Honest, liberal-minded people in the district liked him because they knew he abided by simple uncomplicated rules. Alf Barrett at the Queen Victoria had often explained them to people who didn't know:

'Your freedom to swing your arms stops where Kenny's nose begins.'

Pete, for his part, was known as a bit of a tearaway. The label dated from the time in his fourteenth year when he was implicated in a warehouse theft. For a month after the raid, Dansette record players, canteens of cutlery and ornamental lamps had been turning up at bargain prices all over Walford. Pete was pointed out as one of the juvenile wholesalers by a trader who had turned down some of the goods. Pete was promptly pulled in for questioning.

In the end the police were able to prove nothing, but by that time Pete's reputation was firmly established. Since then he had been in trouble with the law one more time, in connection with a mysteriously-acquired batch of Bob Dylan albums he was offering at half price. His story – that the records had been given to him by a now-departed trader in exchange for work he had done – was reluctantly accepted. No one could be traced who had lost any albums answering that description. In spite of the fact that he had picked up no police convictions over the years, it was still common knowledge in Walford that if you wanted to lay hands on anything cheaper than the trade price, Pete was your man.

Lately, Pete's social profile had changed. He wasn't to be seen much around the old haunts, or in the company of friends like Arthur Fowler and the precocious Den Watts. Instead, he regularly kept the company of Pat Harris, a sultry little blonde that more than a few of the lads had fancied without ever having their longings fulfilled. Where she and Pete spent their evenings, nobody was sure. Everybody was certain, though, that it was very serious between those two.

As the brothers moved away from a window display of hipster trousers and the latest in leather jackets, Kenneth returned to the issue from which Pete had been trying, for five uncomfortable minutes, to move him away.

'There's some things that are bloody hard to go back on,' Kenneth said. 'Best not to take any serious steps until you're a bit older. I know what I'm talkin' about. I made a few decisions that really done me damage.'

One decision Kenneth hadn't made was to get married. He believed a man couldn't make up his mind about anything so serious until he was at least thirty.

'When I was your age, I definitely knew the score. Nobody could tell me different from what I thought. I'd got it all sorted out, Pete. Religion, politics, women, everythin'.' Kenneth snorted now at his early callowness.

'Fat bleedin' lot I knew. Three years later I was regrettin' a lot of the dozey decisions I'd made. I'm *still* stingin' from a couple of them.'

'There's some things you can be sure about at nineteen,' Pete insisted. 'You don't need to have white hair to know it's spot-on you've found the right bird.'

'Like with you an' Pat.' Kenneth groaned. 'Listen, women's minds change after they're twenty, just like blokes'. It's a well-known fact. What she wants now, she won't want then. Same goes for you.'

Pete looked at him. 'You're not goin' to change my mind. Not you nor Mum nor anybody. So you can stop tryin'.'

'Then you must be bleedin' mad, that's all I can say.' Kenneth fired an accurate spit at the gutter. 'What's it all about, anyway? The money you make's enough for you, right? Steady number, bit of overtime, always a few readies in your pocket. But it's not enough to support a wife on. Tight times ahead if you get spliced.'

'We'll manage.'

Kenneth sighed loudly. 'Can't you just settle for a bit of regular nookie? Does it have to be the full ball-an'-chain bit?'

'I like the idea of bein' married,' Pete said.

'Aw, screw the nut, Pete . . .'

'So does Pat. Settlin' down, that's what I'm after. Sortin' my life out an' makin' somethin' of meself. Gettin' married is the start of gettin' settled – Dad always said that.'

'Yeah, well, Dad hadn't come across the likes of Pat Harris, had he?'

Pete stopped, suddenly angry. He grabbed his brother's lapel. 'Just you watch your mouth, Kenny.'

'An' you watch your chin.'

Pete let go. 'Keep your tongue off her, then.'

For three minutes they walked on in moody silence. As they neared the turning that led to Albert Square Kenneth

25

looked at his watch. 'Right,' he said, hard-voiced and businesslike, 'I'm goin' back to my drum. I'll get changed, have a couple or three in the Queen Vic then I'll be round Mum's. What're you doin'?'

'Pickin' up Pat at her place, then I thought we'd have a drink before dinner.'

'Where?'

'The Vic, if it's not goin' to cramp your style.'

'Just keep her out from under my nose, then.'

Peter stared at his brother. 'You can be a right shit when you put your mind to it, know that?'

For the first time in his life, Pete found himself in the position of a man who had overshot the mark with Kenneth. His maroon tie was grabbed so hard he gulped.

'Listen, twat. Your balls are in charge of your brain lately, so I'll make allowances. Anybody else said that, I'd have bopped them.'

'Yeah,' Pete croaked. 'I'm really crappin' meself with fright.'

Kenneth put his face very close. 'Just shut your face an' listen,' he rasped. 'Where that Pat's concerned, you mind your step. Nobody round here knows a toss about her, except that she's a prize cock-teaser. She's learned her stuff out of the district, an' now she's claimin' you for the diploma. I've tried to warn you, Mum's said her bit an' I know Ronnie's not happy. If Harry lived hereabouts he'd be at you about her an' all.'

Pete swallowed hard. His indignation was making way for a surge of emotion. 'You don't understand, any of you. You don't want to.'

Kenneth shook his head, dismissing any likelihood that Pete knew what he was talking about. 'You're makin' a huge mistake. Bear it in mind – you was told.' He released Pete's tie. 'An' just keep her away from me, 'cause I'd sooner be civil to a whore up Frith Street.'

Pete watched Kenneth cross the road, smartly skirting a taxi and bounding lithely on to the far pavement. At that moment Pete felt the way he had the day his dad died. Abandoned. He wanted to grab somebody he could trust and explain it all – how he felt, the warm, lovely sense of belonging that gripped him every time he laid eyes on his girl. Simultaneously, he wanted to reject his entire family.

'Shit on them!' he hissed.

It wasn't fair, any of it. Nobody understood, they were all against Pat because she was so lively and good-looking and they couldn't understand that he *did* know his own mind. To make it right, he should be twenty-eight and she should have a humpty back and a couple of warts on her nose – that way they'd open their arms to her and clap hands at the idea of her becoming Pat Beale.

'Sod them!' He turned and strode off in the direction of Dalton Street where Pat lived. 'Bollocks!' he added, feeling the need for a boost on his exasperation.

As he walked along his feelings softened, gradually, to plain resentment. It was all so sweet and simple, he thought. Nearly the ideal romance. But everybody was trying to make it complicated and sour. He was in love with Pat, that was all, and he wanted her to be his wife. They should be happy for him.

'Women are all right, I suppose,' Terence said. 'But they've always got somethin' up with their muffins.'

Harry Beale nodded. He had the feeling he had come all the way from Bradford just to fall into this trap. Since dinner had finished and the gathering had become casual, Terence had clung to Harry's side like a limpet.

'There's always somethin' the matter, Harry.' Terence narrowed one of his shifty eyes and twitched his pencil-line moustache. 'You're a man now an' I can tell you these things.'

The others were wandering about the house, glasses in hand, laughing and giggling, having a good time of it. Harry sat watching them, trying to ignore his dreaded uncle, the old-time spiv who talked as if he knew what it was like to have the world as his exclusive oyster. He was half drunk, which made him a lot harder to bear than usual.

'I was nearly hitched once, did you know that?'

Harry shook his head, wondering if he should just tell Terence to bugger off. The signs indicated that nothing subtler would have any effect.

'It's true as I'm standin' here – well, sittin'. Big piece she was. Polish. I'd have gone through with it an' all, if she hadn't been eternally sufferin' from some woman's complaint or other.'

Harry decided he'd had enough. He turned to his uncle and said, 'Look, you've got to excuse me. I want to talk to Mum.'

Terence nodded pleasantly. 'Fair enough. See you in a bit.'

Feeling like a fool for not having tried that earlier, Harry got up and went through to the kitchen. His mother was leaning with her back to the sink, sipping a port and lemon and listening to her sister Elsie, who was telling her all about her winter holiday in Malta.

'Just ask Ben,' Elsie was saying. 'There was a place where you could get a slice of cake and a cup of tea just like you get at home.'

Louise was in much the same position as Harry had been until a minute ago. Since three years before, when Elsie's husband had landed a good job with a Middlesex engineering firm, she was forever commending what she called 'the middle-class life' and its adornments.

'Next year, mind you, I think it'll be Ibiza. It's got a lot better tone, I've heard.'

Things had changed for her in a big way. She and her husband had moved into a bigger flat. They had a *five*-piece suite, a shower, fitted carpets and a 21-inch television set, as well as a smart second-hand Rover with artificial leopard-skin seat covers. They took annual holidays abroad and went out for a Chinese meal once a week. It was a full life.

'Oh hello, love!' Louise beamed at Harry, delighted at his intrusion. 'Come an' tell your mum all that's been happenin' since the last time I saw you. What is it you're doin' now anyway?'

As Elsie moved off to corner somebody else, Harry grinned at his mother and pecked her cheek. 'I'm doin' the same as I was doin' five years ago. Seven years ago. Eight . . .'

Harry had been a hotel porter since he left school. Now, he was in charge of twenty porters and other manual staff in one of the largest hotels in Yorkshire.

'But I bet you do it better than anybody else.'

'Of course I do.' He squeezed his mother's arm. 'That was a great dinner,' he said. 'Even if some of them didn't show up.'

'An' one clown came late.'

'My favourite uncle,' Harry grunted. 'What happened to our Dora, by the way?'

'Took the hump. Couldn't go to Clacton because of all that battlin' between the Mods an' Rockers, so she decided she was goin' nowhere. She'll be round that flat of hers right now, shouldn't doubt. Her an' whoever's warmin' her back these days.'

Harry's sense of family was not strong, but he understood how much Dora's behaviour over the past couple of years had hurt his mother.

'She'll sort herself out, one of these days,' he murmured.

'I'll not hold me breath waitin'.' Louise swirled her drink and gazed at it against the light before she sipped. 'I'm not sayin' any of you hurt me deliberately, Harry, but I've been hurt all the same. An' it don't get no better lately.'

Most of the small plans and hopes Louise had clung to after Albert's death had disintegrated, one by one. The

29

most cherished plans of all centred on the family and how they would set about making their own separate lives. Louise had expected them to marry in order, the oldest first and so on down to the youngest, Pete and Pauline. So far, the only one who had married was Ronnie. Dora, Harry and Kenneth, who were all older, showed no inclination to settle down yet. The only one keen on the idea was Pete.

'I might make you proud of me, yet,' Harry said.

'I'm proud of you as it is.' Louise reached out and gently pinched his cheek.

'I've been seein' this girl, regular like. If it works out, I'll bring her to meet you.'

Louise's mouth became a small oval, like a child anticipating a treat. 'That'd be lovely. Lovely. From Yorkshire, is she?'

'No. London born an' bred. She's a receptionist at the place where I work.'

Harry could see he had done a lot, at a stroke, to brighten his mother's day. And it would give her something to look forward to. She was good at clinging to hopes and expectations, in spite of all her bleak experience.

'You see you bring her next time you come down.'

'I'll do my best.'

It was enough to leave her with that much – the knowledge, the promise, the expectation. There was no point telling her the rest – that his girlfriend was married, had a child, and was such a heavy drinker she was barely able to hold down her job. Harry decided to change the subject, if not the broad topic.

'I see Pete brought his young lady to grace the gatherin',' he said.

Louise's cheerful expression switched quickly to a scowl. 'Young lady? Dressed like that? Young trollope, more like.'

'They all wear mini skirts now, Mum.'

30

'They don't all go flashin' their knickers every chance they get. I thought our Terry's eyes'd drop out.'

Harry laughed. 'I don't think he likes women, much.'

'He don't like responsibility, whatever shape it takes.'

At that moment, out in the hallway, Terence was being strongly discouraged by Pete's girlfriend, Pat, who was disturbed, among other things, by his habit of glancing at her knees every few seconds as he talked. He was a creepy little man, she thought.

'Do you think you'll be votin', yourself?' Terence enquired.

'I don't know anythin' about politics,' she told him coldly. She was sitting on a cushion on the floor, trying to make her legs invisible beneath her. 'They're borin', anyway.'

'Not when you really get into the subject.' Terence assured her, his eyes still skating across her polished kneecaps.

'Really?' The frost was almost visible.

Terence had asked Pat what she thought would be the probable outcome of the first elections, in April, for the Greater London Council. To Terence's way of thinking, that was a pretty sharp question to ask a girl. It showed he was in touch with things.

'I don't think Labour stands an earthly,' he ploughed on. 'To a lifelong Tory like meself – '

'Where have you been?' Pat demanded sharply.

Terence gaped at her, confused, then realized she was addressing Pete, who had detached himself from the crowd in the front room.

'I was just talkin',' Pete said. 'You know, circulatin'.'

Pat stood up. 'I want to go home.'

Pete gave her a pained look. 'Not yet, love. We can't just eat an' then take off.'

'You stop if you like. I'm goin'.'

Terence made a silent withdrawal as Pete began shifting his feet. 'I wanted you to have a word with Mum before you go. A proper word – you know, talk to her about things.'

Pat narrowed her dark-lined eyes. 'Get her to like me, you mean?'

'Let her know what you're like. She hardly knows anythin' about you. Only what I've told her.'

Pat made a slow circle on the carpet with the toe of her scarlet shoe. 'Have you told her when we're gettin' married?'

Pete shook his head. 'Haven't had a chance.'

'So you haven't told her why, either?'

'She's known a long time that I want to marry you.' Pete looked over his shoulder to see if anyone was listening. 'The other thing – well, that don't make any difference, far as I'm concerned. It's one more reason, that's all. I wanted to marry you before that.' He fidgeted. 'Will you come through an' have a word with her? Hmm?'

Pat said no without making a sound or moving a muscle.

Pete sighed and looked at the front door. 'All right. If you really have to go, I'll come with you. But Pat . . .'

'What?'

'Come round tomorrow, eh? You've got to get to know each other better. It's only right.'

Pat took her coat from the hallstand. 'I'll come round, Pete, as long as she's got no crowd backin' her up, an' as long as she knows just where she stands in all this. It's you I'm marryin', not her.'

Pete's eyes begged a little compassion. 'What makes you think she's goin' to have a go at you?'

'You told me yourself, she don't want us to get married. An' I caught her lookin' at me when we were eatin' our dinner. She don't like me an' she never will.' She slid the coat over her shoulders and stepped close to Pete. 'I don't need her blessin,' she said quietly. 'An' you'd best get used to livin' without it, too.'

32

Glumly, Pete followed her to the door, wondering why there had to be so many obstacles in the way of being happy.

3

'Your visit seems to have put a lasting glow in the heart of Vera Taylor,' Harold Legg read; 'When I was down again on Sunday she wanted to know all manner of things about you. Before I left, she asked that I should remember her to you.'

Matchmakers, Harold thought. He was beset by them. His mother and sister never stopped finding prospects for him – always nice Jewish girls, of course – and Ethel Skinner, who lived with her husband in one of Harold's flats upstairs, had lectured him a time or two on how unnatural it was for a man to live alone. Now Roger was at the same game.

He sat tapping his fingers absently on the desk for a moment, trying to remember Vera Taylor. Roger had a lot of women friends in Eastbourne and Harold suspected he was very intimate with two or three of them. Vera Taylor, if he remembered correctly, wasn't one of that group. She was in her thirties, tall, demure and rather scholarly. She was the kind of woman who called to mind the colour brown.

Harold glanced up at the clock. It was time to begin morning surgery. He put Roger Lewis's letter aside and tapped the bell on the desk. The door opened a moment later and Reg Cox shuffled in.

'Mornin', Doctor.'

'Good morning, Reg. Come and sit down.'

The shabby, sallow-skinned man traversed the few feet from the door to the desk as if it were a desert. His legs seemed only just capable of supporting him. He gripped the back of the chair and crab-walked himself to where he could sit. The lowering action was a masterpiece of slow motion.

'I've come about another prescription,' he said. His watery eyes avoided Harold's.

Harold consulted the case card in front of him. 'You had one only last week. That was a fortnight's supply.'

The lie, when it came, was delivered with all the shiftiness good liars learn to avoid. 'I knocked the bottle over into the sink. The lid was off an' the pills got soaked. They was just one big lump by the time I fished the bottle out.'

There were already three red query marks on the card. They each denoted a time when Reg's prescription had run out early, for one alleged reason or another. Harold never allowed more than three red queries to appear before he took corrective action.

'To be frank with you,' he said, 'I think it'd be a good thing if you stayed off the tablets for a week, anyway.'

Reg's torpor slipped. His head jerked back. 'But I need them.'

'Let me be the judge of that, eh? Phenobarbitone can be habit-forming, Reg. It's not a drug you should stay on any longer than necessary.'

'But I can't sleep without them. The pains – '

'You weren't given them for the pains, or to make you sleep. They're to stabilize your seizures.' Reg had sustained severe injuries from a bad fall during the war. Since then he had suffered from a minor type of epilepsy, as well as arthritis in his legs and arms. 'I take it you didn't knock your arthritis pills into the sink,' Harold added.

Reg shook his head. 'I do need them pills,' he mumbled. 'I feel funny if I don't take them.'

'You'd feel a lot funnier if you were to go on swallowing them at the present rate.'

Reg tried to look maligned. 'I took them just like it said on the bottle.'

Harold flattened his hands before him on the desk, letting it be known he would stand no nonsense. 'I'm taking you off the tablets for a week. Come back this time next week and I'll let you have some more. A different kind.'

'Different?'

'They do the same job.' And you don't wind up like an opium addict, Harold thought. Epanutin wasn't as powerful as phenobarbitone, but in the case of someone like Reg Cox it was obviously the safer bet.

'Right.' Reg looked sorely disgruntled. He hoisted himself to his feet. 'Lord knows how I'm goin' to sleep at nights . . .'

'Try the way you used to do it. Two or three pints of Luxford and Copley's before bedtime.'

Harold watched Reg go; he didn't miss the rebuke implicit in the way the door was banged shut. It was hard to be sympathetic towards Reg. He abused sympathy, just as he abused everything else that was offered. In the past he had fiddled the National Assistance Board, robbed his gas meter – although he swore it was done by intruders – he had falsified insurance documents relating to the ownership of the old van he drove, and Harold was certain he had once lifted a paper knife off his desk. The man was, moreover, thoroughly anti-social in his day-to-day behaviour. There was little about Reg that invited anyone to try and like him. Those who did try always failed miserably.

Harold rang the bell again and smiled as Louise Beale came in. They exchanged greetings and she sat down. Harold waited for the usual clear, explicit statement of her complaint. This morning, however, she seemed to be stuck for words.

'Is it the joints again, Lou?' he prompted.

'That's right. Actin' up rotten.' She rubbed her arm. 'Me right leg's a bit stiff an' all.'

'Do you still take regular walks, as I suggested?'

She nodded.

'Exercise is very important. Exercise and warmth.' He watched her carefully for a moment. 'What's really up, Lou?'

She made a face at the desk.

'You did come about something else, didn't you?'

'That Pete of mine,' she grunted.

'What's wrong with him?'

'Must've blew his brains out into his hankie, if you ask me.'

Harold nodded. 'I see. You mean you're upset about him wanting to get married?'

'Oh. You've heard, then.'

'It would have been hard not to. It's quite a talking point around the square. What do you think I can do to help – or did you just want to talk about it?'

Lou clasped her fingers in front of her handbag. 'I'm stuck for a way to make him see sense,' she said. 'I've tried bein' gentle about it. I explained that if he just waits a while he'll be surer, or he'll change his mind. Now isn't the time for him to be doin' this, I said.'

'A sensible approach,' Harold murmured.

'It done me no good. So I tried puttin' me foot down. That was useless an' all. I've tried the lot.'

'I'm sure you have.' Harold had seen Louise in action. She had a formidably wide range of techniques for persuading people.

'Bad enough he wants to get wed – but that girl . . . Well. She was round one night last week. Dolled up like a tart. If her heart's as hard as her face, the man that lands her's in for some stick.'

Harold tried to look sympathetic.

'She sat an' laid the law down to me in my own front room. Said they was gettin' married at the beginnin' of May, an they'd be movin' into a couple of rooms at the top of her mum's house. All cut an' dried. As if I'd no say in any of it. All Pete did was sit there an' nod. When

37

I tackled him about her later on, he said he didn't want to hear a word said against her. Imagine.'

'So he's determined. There's nothing harder to shift than a young mind that's made up.'

'His dad would have managed it.'

'Yes, if anyone could, it would have been Albert.' Harold remembered the way Pete always followed his father around, practically from the time he could walk. When Albert died the boy had been inconsolable for days.

'The thought of it burns me,' Louise sighed. 'Why wasn't Albert spared, when the likes of that Reg Cox is still knockin' about?'

Harold said nothing to fill the questioning silence. Whatever Louise's reasons for disliking Reg, they were a shade stronger than most people's.

'One word from Albert,' she said eventually, 'an' Pete would have toed the line. One word.' She sighed again. 'I never saw a kid so attached to his dad. Do you remember, when Albert came home from war, he wasn't able to smoke fags any more, so he took up the pipe?'

'Yes.'

'Pete's still got them pipes. All six of them. He even takes them out an' handles them when he thinks nobody's lookin'.' She narrowed her eyes. 'I know what it is. They've still got that strong tobacco smell. It reminds him of his dad. The one man in all the world he really looked up to . . .'

'Lou, listen,' Harold said gently. 'It's no use torturing yourself with regret. If there's an answer to your problem, it doesn't lie in the direction of "if only". Do you want me to have a word with Pete?'

'It might help if you did . . .'

'I'll be frank with you – I don't think it will. But I'll see him anyway. Tell him to come over tonight, about seven.'

'Thanks. Thanks very much.' Louise stood up.

'Now do you want me to give you something for your joints?'

She looked at him blankly for a moment, then shook her head. 'No, I don't need nothin' for them.' She went to the door and opened it. 'They're fine, this time of year.'

In the following ninety minutes Harold saw eleven more patients. After a short coffee break he set out to do his house rounds. As he was unlocking the car door Pauline Beale came by. She was carrying a parcel with the bright orange label of the steam laundry where she worked.

'Have they got you doing deliveries now?' Harold asked her.

'No. Just this one. It's for old Mrs Trevor. She can't get about much.'

'It looks heavy.'

'It is. She saves up the washin' for a month then gets it all done at once.' She flashed her pretty, open smile. 'I don't mind. It's a good excuse to get away from the laundry for a bit.' She stood by as Harold put his bag on the passenger seat.

'Has Mum been to see you? About Pete?'

Harold unfolded himself from the interior of the car. 'Yes, she has.'

'She said she was goin' to.'

Harold examined her frown. Like her mother, whom she resembled, young Pauline had a very expressive face. 'What's up?' Harold said. 'Don't you think I should speak to him?'

'No, it's not that. I just wish Mum would give in. It's goin' to be less of a strain on her if she does. All this upset's for nothin'.'

'You don't think Pete'll be persuaded to change his mind?'

'Not by anybody.' Pauline glanced along the street. 'The thing is . . .' She looked at Harold. 'Well, Pat, the girl he wants to marry, she's pregnant. He'll stand by her, no matter what.'

Harold's heart sank a little. 'And your mother doesn't know?'

'No. I only found out because one of her mates let it slip to a girl that works in the laundry.'

'Thanks for telling me. If I'm going to talk to Pete, it's as well for me to have as many facts as I can, in advance.' He glanced along by the Queen Victoria. A young man in a boiler suit was standing there, nervously kicking at the pavement with the stubby toe of his work boot. 'I think Arthur Fowler's waiting to have a word, Pauline.'

'Oh.' Pauline tutted. 'Him.'

'I've always thought he was a nice, steady young man.'

'I suppose he is. But he's no Stewart Grainger, is he?'

'Perhaps not.' Harold ducked down and got into the car. 'It can be a harsh world for people with dreams, can't it?' He smiled as she waved and walked away.

That night Pete came into the front room and sat opposite his mother. She was alone, reading her daily paper. As Pete sat staring across at her she continued to read for a minute, then slowly lifted her head.

'Well? Have you been to see Dr Legg?'

Pete nodded.

'So what have you come to tell me?'

'We're still goin' through with it.'

Louise stared at him, taking in his face feature by feature – the steady eyes, the aggressively hooked nose, the stubborn angle of his chin. His father's boy, every inch.

'You're set on breakin' my heart, aren't you?'

'No Mum, I'm not. You know I'm not.'

'Didn't the doctor say *anythin*' to make you think again?'

'Not really.'

What the doctor had offered was reassurance. First, he

had warned Pete about the uphill struggle ahead of him, of the need he would sometimes have for counsel. Then he went on to tell Pete about Uncle Leon, who sounded like a marvellous man. Dr Legg's uncle had died not long ago. He had been the doctor's friend, adviser, companion and comforter. Dr Legg had told Pete to look on him as an Uncle Leon. At a time when he badly needed someone to confide in, it was an offer that had moved Pete close to tears.

'If your father was here . . .'

'Mum.'

'This is no way to treat his memory, Pete . . .'

'Mum. Listen.' Dr Legg had told him to let her know without delay or hesitation. 'Pat's pregnant. She's goin' to have my baby.'

Louise's eyes widened and seemed to freeze that way. 'Why didn't you tell me?'

'I wanted to, but I didn't know how you'd take it . . .'

'You ruddy young fool.'

'I suppose I am.'

'You should have told me straight away.' She folded her paper and stuck it down the side of the chair. 'Put the weddin' off for two more weeks. To the end of May.'

Pete looked bewildered. 'What?'

'It'll take that long to make proper arrangements.' She shook her head at him. 'There's no undoin' what's done. So we make the best of it. Bring Pat round here an' we'll talk about who's to be invited an' who's not.' She paused, then said, 'Tell her, an' all, that from now on she's welcome in this house. She's goin' to be one of us, after all.'

It was a long time later, as he lay wide-awake in bed, that Pete finally understood. His mother had never been any different. In any family dispute, whether she won or lost, she stood by her principles. Louise Beale was known for always doing the right thing by her own.

He smiled as, for the first time in weeks, he began to

slide into an easy sleep. He should have known how she would react to his news, he thought dreamily. He would bet Dr Legg had known.

4

Kathy Hills was only seventeen, but it could already be said she'd had a hard life. She came from the poor end of Walford, from one of the poorest of the poor families. Her father was a drunkard who was regularly violent towards Kathy and her mother. She had five brothers who were always in trouble and always about the place; she had never known what it was like to have a room of her own, or even to be alone in the house.

At school Kathy had worn the shabbiest uniform; she had never had enough money to do the casual things – going to coffee bars, buying sweets or a magazine – that other schoolgirls did all the time. Even now, with a job in the packing bay at a department store, she was left with hardly anything to spend on herself, because her father demanded three-quarters of her wage to cover rent and food.

But Kathy never felt sorry for herself. She endured her life by always looking towards a horizon bright with everything she had so far been denied. She had plans, hopes, dreams; they cushioned her way along the trough of disadvantage and hardship.

On a Saturday towards the end of May, however, Kathy stood at the roadside and watched the cancellation of one of her most cherished dreams. Across the road, in the doorway of Walford Parish Church, Pete Beale stood with his new bride on his arm, smiling as family and friends clustered round, throwing confetti and taking snapshots.

'She looks nice, doesn't she?' Kathy's diminutive friend, Lottie Bright, was touched by the event, although she had reservations. 'When I get married it won't be in blue, though. An' it'll be a proper wedding dress.'

Kathy wasn't listening. She was staring at Pat Harris – now Pat Beale – wondering what awful spell she'd worked, what ugly temptations she'd used to remove Pete from the meticulously planned schedule of her future.

'He looks really smart. Then he always was, wasn't he?'

Kathy glanced at Lottie. 'What?'

'Pete Beale. He's always been a smart looker.'

Kathy watched him smile hammily for the clicking cameras. A smart looker. He was a lot more than that. To her he had represented everything she could want in a husband. For years she had studied him, delighting silently in what he was. She knew his mannerisms, his style of speech, every outward characteristic. In reverie, more times than she could count, Kathy had made herself his counterpart, the girl who fitted into the picture of confidence and jaunty charm. Without making any hard plans towards the fulfillment of that dream, she was nevertheless certain it would come true. Faith was everything. All of seven years ago she had ordained herself his soul mate, his partner for life.

She had tried to prepare herself for the shock, for the moment when it would be certain that he was out of her future. But she hadn't been able to believe it would happen. Today she had come along hoping to learn that the marriage was off, that there was a last-minute change of heart, preferably on his part. But there they were, the newly-weds. It was all over.

'You used to fancy him a bit, didn't you?' Lottie said impishly. 'You was always followin' him about at school.'

'That was a long time ago,' Kathy pointed out. Since those days she had kept her idolatry beneath the surface. From puberty she clung to the belief that an abiding, unspoken admiration for Pete Beale would, somehow, draw more of his attention than her flirting ever did.

44

As she watched the couple get into the shiny hired car, a new, much less poetic hope reared from the ashes of the dead one.

'It won't last.' She hadn't meant to say it out loud.

Lottie frowned at her. 'Why not?'

'She's wrong for him.'

'My Mum an' Dad are wrong for each other. So's yours. Lots of married people are badly matched. They stick it, though, don't they? They learn to put up with things.'

'He's not the kind to stick it.' She was formulating the reasons as she went, re-shaping her future as solidly as likelihood would permit. 'Too much spirit in him.'

Lottie shrugged. 'They look happy enough to me.'

As the car swept away from the church Pete looked out of the window. For an instant his eyes were on Kathy. She snatched that slice of time and planted it in the gap on her horizon; his eyes and hers, locked, belonging on each other.

The reception was held in one of the bars at the Queen Victoria. Alf and Polly Barrett had put covers on the tables and set out plates of Polly's speciality; 'I call it my finger buffet,' she explained to a trio of Pat's relatives, two women and a man, who were huffily surveying the piles of sausage rolls, chicken drumsticks, vol-au-vent and little triangular sandwiches.

'It's not a sit-down do, then,' one of the women muttered. 'I never think it's a proper weddin', without a knife-an'-fork dinner.'

The guests, thirty in all, were expected to buy their own drinks, after the initial glass of wine for the toasts. In the event, no toasts were made. The best man had indulged heavily at the stag party the night before. He was still semi-drunk at the church ceremony. The first thing he did when he arrived at the Queen Victoria was to sink two pints to slake his murderous thirst. The beer set the accumulated alcohol moving faster in his system. By the time someone suggested he propose the toast to the bride and groom, he was already past the point where he could speak coherently. So were a lot of the others. Formalities were abandoned.

Pete and his bride, standing at the end of the room, were noticeably subdued. They made polite conversation when people spoke to them, but whenever they were left on their own they fell silent. Pete eventually realized that people were noticing. He turned to Pat, forcing a wide smile.

'We're puttin' the mockers on things,' he murmured. 'Try an' brighten up a bit.'

'You do it for both of us,' she snapped. 'I don't feel like bein' bright.'

'Christ.'

Pete looked around. The families weren't mingling. They were cheerful enough, most of them, but they were distributed about the bar in tight partisan clusters. Only the friends, most of them people the couple had grown up with, were showing democratic tendencies. Parents, aunts, uncles, cousins, brothers and sisters were all keeping strictly to their born kin.

Pete turned back to Pat. Today he hardly recognized her. A few times over the months she had been moody, but now she behaved as if she were having two headaches at once. She even looked different; her hair had been arranged in a high, off-the-forehead style and her lipstick was much paler than usual. She had done something different to her eyes, too.

'What is it, anyway?'

'You know what it is.'

Pete smiled and waved across to his Aunt Queenie. 'You still on about Clacton?' he demanded through clenched teeth.

'Yeah. Clacton. Some surprise honeymoon.'

He had told her about Clacton on the way back from

the church. Since then Pat had been stiff to the point of rigor.

'I thought you'd like it there.'

'I fancied up North somewhere. Blackpool. Southport. Even Morecambe would've been better than Clacton. I told you the places I liked.'

'But you said you'd leave the arrangements to me. You *wanted* me to surprise you.'

Pat was watching Louise Beale attempting to make conversation with her mother. Mrs Harris was responding, but she managed to keep up an expression that suggested she was demeaning herself.

'You did leave it to me, didn't you?' Pete insisted.

'We're only going to Clacton because that's where you used to go with your Dad.'

Pete was about to deny that, then decided not to. 'So what? It's a nice place, as nice as any.'

'We'll most likely get done over by a bunch of Rockers.'

'Don't be silly.' He squeezed her arm. 'Come on, love. Cheer up. This is your big day.'

'Oh yeah,' she said, stony-faced. 'So it is.'

In a corner of the bar, wielding a pint of bitter, Pete's young friend Den Watts was preparing to make an impression on Angie Shaw. Angie was seventeen, three years older than Den, and already she had the sparkly good looks and coquettish style that could guarantee her a following wherever she went.

Den had been watching her since he came in. Her wide, candid eyes and firm little body created a witch-angel effect on him that set his glands singing. By degrees he had sidled over to where she was talking with another of Pete's friends, Arthur Fowler. It was difficult cutting himself into their conversation, but Den believed he was managing it well enough.

'I always thought Pete would be the last of us to get married,' Arthur was saying. 'It was a bit of a shock when he told me he an' Pat was goin' to tie the knot.'

47

Arthur was twenty-two, a short, stocky, square-faced man with dark, swept-back hair who always gave the impression of being older than he was. He dressed much more traditionally than the rest of his friends and was a great believer in the orderly life.

'I mean,' he went on, 'he was a right lad – never settlin' to anythin', always tearin' about. At one time he never stayed with the same girlfriend longer than a week.'

'Yeah, it's quite a turn up, this weddin',' Den said.

Angie stared at him for a second, then returned her attention to Arthur. 'When're you gettin' married, then?' She winked at him. 'Got somebody lined up, have you?'

Arthur's eyes were tempted to wander to Pauline Beale, but he kept them on Angie. 'I might have. Nothin' planned yet, mind you.'

'Not sayin' who it is?'

'Arthur's too close to give anythin' away,' Den observed. 'Him an' me know the value of keepin' our secrets. Right, Arthur?'

Again Angie looked at Den. This time she was inspecting him. She had known him for years, without really taking any notice. Tall, eager-eyed, a sharp dresser. 'You've got a lot of secrets, have you?'

Den sipped his pint, simultaneously lowering one eyelid. 'I'll say.'

'I'd have thought you was too young,' Angie remarked cuttingly. 'A bit young for that pint, too.'

'When you're big enough,' Den drawled, 'you're old enough.'

'Ooh.' Angie rolled her eyes. 'So you reckon you're a real big boy, do you?'

'Give me the chance,' Den promised with a leer, 'an' I'll show you just *how* big.'

Arthur had spotted Pauline on her own by one of the tables, trying to make up her mind what to eat. 'See you in a bit,' he murmured to Den and Angie as he moved away.

Pauline was adding a sausage roll to the collection on her plate when Arthur stepped up beside her. 'Can I get you a drink?'

She smiled tightly at him. 'No thanks, Arthur. I've got one.'

'Have a spare, then.'

She mustered a second refusal, then she swallowed it and nodded. 'All right. It's a vodka and lime.'

He stared at her. 'I didn't know you drank vodka.'

'I'm givin' it a try,' she said, flashing the smile that always put a little pang through his heart. 'It's a weddin', isn't it? Anythin' goes.'

When Arthur came back with the drink Pauline offered him one of the sandwiches on her plate. He didn't want one but he took it, nevertheless. 'Enjoyin' yourself?' he asked her lightly.

'Yes. You?'

'Yes, I'm enjoyin' it.'

In every exchange they had – they were always contrived by Arthur – the conversation failed to flow. It tended, rather, to limp from one blind alley to another. Pauline had come to a point where she sometimes avoided Arthur, although she didn't dislike him. She didn't really object to the fact that he obviously fancied her, either. He just put such a strain on her, trying to think of things to say.

After making a great show of relishing the sandwich, Arthur wiped the crumbs from his mouth and said, 'When does it pack in? The reception, I mean?'

'It'll just fizzle out,' Pauline told him. 'They usually do, don't they?'

'Hmm. I was wonderin' – I mean, are you stoppin' late, or would you fancy maybe coming to the pictures?'

Pauline noted the breakthrough. He had never actually asked her out before, although he had been on the verge a few times. She considered his proposition. 'Well. I don't know if Mum expects me to stop or what.'

49

Arthur was surprised she was even considering it. He had swiftly prepared himself to accept a refusal gracefully, and to suggest they do it another time.

'There's a couple of good ones on,' he said. 'At the Essoldo they've got 'Lord of the Flies', and 'Goldfinger''s on at the Gaumont.'

'Hang on.' Pauline went off and spoke to her mother, who was talking to Harry and Kenneth. When she came back she was nodding. 'All right,' she said, making Arthur's heart rise. 'If you don't mind hanging back a bit, we can go straight from here.'

'Fine,' he gulped.

'Can we make it 'Goldfinger'? I love Sean Connery.'

'Anything you want,' Arthur said, meaning it in a sense so wide it would have made Pauline's head spin.

From where he stood, Harry saw Arthur start grinning pinkly. 'Reckon Pauline's made Arthur's day,' he observed.

Louise didn't hear him. She had simply paused for breath in her round condemnation of the Harris family. 'It fair cuts me up, to think our Pete's goin' to be livin' with that lot.'

'He'll be all right,' Kenneth assured her. 'They ain't a bad crowd, really.'

'That mum of theirs is a right hoity-toity cow. Puttin' on airs an' graces just because one of her lads works in a drawin' office.'

Harry, whose private life in Bradford was going rather better lately, was in a mood to make allowances. 'You'd be the same, Mum. Pride. Mothers can't help burstin' with it.'

'I wouldn't go on like her, I wouldn't.' Louise took a fierce gulp from her glass. 'Thinks she's the whole cheese, when she's only the smell.'

Kenneth and Harry looked at each other and laughed.

The afternoon drifted by. Tiny conflicts arose and were resolved. Friends re-affirmed their unity and strangers smiled at one another. Pete and his new bride began to relax. Trite philosophies were aired, some of them tearfully, as the men got drunker. A few new friendships were forged.

As the bride and groom prepared to leave, friends and relatives clustered around the taxi, sprinkling the remainder of the confetti, shouting their good wishes. As the fresh air collided with the overload of beer he had taken, Den Watts had to rush back into the pub and head for the toilets. Angie Shaw, watching his retreat, decided that although he was still a bit of a raw kid, she liked him. He would amount to something in her life, if she ever decided to let him.

As the taxi pulled away Pete sat back and let out a long, grateful sigh. 'Thank God for that.' He grinned at Pat. 'It's done an' over with, Mrs Beale.'

She smiled and leaned closer to him.

'Are you sure Clacton's goin' to be all right? I mean, maybe I could change the arrangements, if you don't really think you're going' to enjoy yourself.'

'Oh, I'll enjoy myself, all right.' she murmured. Her hand crept along his thigh. 'An' since I'm goin' to be enjoyin' myself so much, it don't really matter where we go, does it?'

Pete buried his face in her shoulder, inhaling her perfume and thanking God he had made it at long last. *He had married his Pat!* With that golden fact glowing in him, warm and bright, he swore there would be no stopping him now. He was going to take life by the horns.

5

Towards the end of 1964, Harold Legg began to understand what older people meant when they talked about
time just slipping away. The year had seemed impossibly
short, as if a few months had been removed from the
calendar in the interests of efficiency.

So short a year, yet so much had happened. Harold's
memory, which had always marshalled facts like an auto-
matic, ever-expanding encyclopedia, was crammed with
events. It had been the year when a Labour Government
took control in Britain after thirteen years of Conservative
administration; it was the year, too, when the Russians
walked off with 41 medals at the Tokyo Olympics, while
Britain took only five; Cassius Clay beat Sonny Liston in
the World Heavyweight Championship fight; Brezhnev
replaced Kruschev; British Members of Parliament voted
themselves a salary of £3,250 a year; and the BBC
launched its second television channel. The Daily Herald
had made its last appearance in September and was
replaced, next day, by The Sun.

No amount of facts, though, could alter Harold's
impression of time accelerating. Even in uneventful per-
iods the hours flew. He began to suffer the classical,
bewildering sensation of work expanding and time being
telescoped. He was no busier than he had been a year
before, yet he felt he was working twice as hard just to
keep up.

He supposed he was entering middle-age, if only the
ante-room. There was some grey in his hair and the
suggestion of slackness at the jaw. He no longer leapt up
steps the way he once did, nor was he able, very often, to
stay awake in front of the television set after ten o'clock.

As Christmas passed and the grey tail-end of winter made it seem that time, after all, wasn't really moving so fast, Harold's father began talking about retirement. He was in his mid-sixties and although he was still a very fit man, he wanted time to write his textbook on heart disease, a project which, he said, he had put off for too many years.

Father and son had been working together at Gregory Legg's consulting rooms, one day a fortnight, for ten years. Harold's flair for cardiology had been kept nourished and his knowledge had grown steadily. Lately, by dropping remarks that were something more than hints, Gregory had made it clear that he now viewed his son as his successor. Harold had done nothing to encourage his father's hopes in that direction, but an evening came, in March, when he knew it would be necessary to apply a little discouragement.

They were in the study at Harold's parents' home in Finchley. Gregory had once said that when Harold left in the early forties the house seemed to grow larger. When his sister moved out three years later, it became positively vast.

Often, since Judith's death, Gregory had tried to persuade Harold to go back and live there. It was roomy, after all, much brighter and more convenient than the flat he had in Islington. Each time the suggestion was made Harold had declined, without going into painful explanations. The fact was, he simply couldn't live with his mother, whose mania for the Jewish faith would have smothered him in a house twice the size.

'I asked you round because there are decisions that can't be put off any longer,' Gregory explained as he handed Harold a glass of sherry. 'They involve you, to a large extent.'

Harold watched his father, feeling a surge of warmth as the tall, dark-suited man sat down behind his desk and rested his hands on the worn leather inlay. His hair was completely white now, enriching his permanent air of gentleness and dignity. His eyes, in particular, evoked a compassionate understanding that had grown from forty years of caring deeply about his patients, and his profession. *I love you Father*, Harold thought, *but I'm going to have to hurt you.*

'As from the end of this month,' Gregory said, 'I'm taking one year to withdraw gracefully from the practice.'

'A lot of people are going to miss you.'

'And I shall miss them. I'd be consoled, though, to know they were in hands I could trust.'

Harold nodded. 'There's no shortage of good cardiologists in London, Father.'

'I had hoped to keep the practice in the family, so to speak . . .'

Harold set his glass down carefully on the edge of the desk. 'Cardiology's like recreation to me,' he said. 'I never wanted to get into it full time.'

Gregory frowned. 'Why not? You have a talent for the work. It interests you, and you have a lot to offer.'

'I'm an East End GP. I'm interested in that work, too, and I believe I've a lot to offer there. The difference is dedication. If I've got any at all, it lies with my little flock in Walford. I couldn't bring that sort of commitment to your practice, Father.'

Gregory sighed. 'There are many, many doctors who could do the job you do now. Your patients wouldn't come to any harm if another general practitioner took over your patch.'

'Something in me might come to harm if I moved out. I'd honestly rather stay.'

'If you did that,' Gregory countered, 'you'd be denying your skill the opportunity to flower.'

'But not my spirit,' Harold said, 'if you'll pardon me for bringing emotion into my argument. My patients, the quality of life where I work – they fulfil me. Now I'm sure I could keep up most of the standards you've set for your practice, but I wouldn't be all that happy.'

'I see,' Gregory murmured.

Harold saw the sadness gather behind his father's eyes. 'I'm not saying all this to be difficult. I don't like to hurt you or disappoint you. I'm trying to tell you that I'm where I belong.' Judith had crystallized it perfectly, in two words, when they had first decided they would live in Albert Square; 'Everything fits,' she'd said.

Gregory sat in silence for a moment, gazing at the gilt inkstand on the desk, his eyes troubled. Finally he sat back and looked at Harold. 'I won't say I didn't expect a little resistance, but I hadn't foreseen that your stance would be so firm.' He drummed his fingers. 'You've taken the wind out of my sails, Harold. I was all set for a long discussion of ways and means.' He leaned forward again. 'Will you promise me something?'

'What?'

'Think about it. Nothing, apart from death, is as final or fixed as we believe it is. Not when we take time to examine it closely, without haste. To use a frequent remark of your mother's – search your heart.'

'Very well,' Harold promised. 'I'll do that.'

Gregory stood up. 'Remember to take your time.'

Harold said he would. They left the study a few minutes later and went to the sitting room. Harold's mother was there, as they had expected, but there was another woman, too. Gregory was obviously surprised to see her. As he glanced at Harold his eyes telegraphed a heavy apology.

'Ah, here they are,' Mrs Legg beamed. She crossed the room in a swirl of tulle, her high, silvery hair glinting as she stood on tiptoe and kissed Harold's cheek. 'Here's somebody I want you to meet,' she gushed, taking him by the arm. The woman stood up as Mrs Legg dragged Harold towards her. 'My son Harold. Harold, this is Jessica Gilbert.'

'How do you do,' Harold said stiffly.

'A pleasure,' Jessica smiled.

Over the years they got no better, Harold reflected, these women his mother kept hurling at him. This one was perhaps thirty-five, bulky and square-featured, with bulbous eyes and thick dark-brown hair that appeared to start unnaturally low on her forehead. She was trying to look sweet-natured and demure, but Harold, who was used to reading faces, detected a submerged harshness in her.

'Jessica is a writer, Harold. In her spare time she teaches Hebrew at night school.'

'You must be very gifted,' Harold said. 'I can't even cope with Yiddish.'

'I'm sure Jessica could teach you,' his mother trilled.

'Are you a friend of mother's then? She didn't tell me she knew any writers.'

He saw the slight fluster cross Jessica's face, leaving its pink wake on her cheeks. 'We've only just met, actually . . .'

'I was introduced to Jessica at a charity gathering in the synagogue,' his mother said hastily. 'I asked her to drop by this evening for a chat.'

How, Harold wondered, could the woman let this be done to her? How could she do it to herself, for that matter, submitting to being thrust at a succession of single men who either didn't want to get married, or who were as hard-up for charm as she was? It was doubly annoying to Harold. He didn't want to marry again, and if he had wanted to, he would have let something happen, he wouldn't have got mixed up in anything so bizarre as a cold-blooded matching session.

His mother made her next move with even less subtlety than usual. 'Gregory, there's something I'd like your opinion about. If you wouldn't mind coming into the next room for a moment . . .' She turned to Harold and Jessica. 'Why don't you two have a nice chat? Get to

56

know one another. We won't be long.' Gregory was whisked out of the room and the door was firmly shut.

A knot of anger clutched Harold's stomach as he indicated to Jessica that she should sit down again. He remained standing, looking at her in silence, aware that she was expecting him to set the conversation in motion. Her colour rose again. He was making her very uncomfortable. That was good, Harold thought. This one and his mother both needed to be taught a lesson.

'Ah . . . what interests do you have, Harold, when you're not busy at your profession?'

'Not many interests, really,' he said casually. 'What about you?'

'Oh, I've lots of interests, in spite of the demands my work makes on my time.'

'What kind of writer are you, anyway?'

'I write articles for magazines. Mostly about our religion and culture.'

Harold would have put money on it. 'I can imagine that keeps you busy.'

'Oh, it does.' She emitted a short, shrill giggle, as if she had said something funny. 'In my spare time, apart from teaching that is, I paint. I do dressmaking. I'm a very keen cook, too.' It sounded, Harold reflected, like a list of answers on a marriage-bureau application form. 'Music, I *adore* music. And poetry.'

'Poetry? Do you know Larkin, at all?'

She frowned. 'I don't think so.'

'Philip Larkin. He isn't prolific, mind you. It takes him years to produce enough stuff to fill a very thin volume.'

'Perhaps he'll improve.'

Harold made a mental eye-roll. 'What poets do you like?'

She thought for a moment. 'Zalman Shneour,' she said eventually. 'Bialik, and I'm very fond of Nathan Alterman.'

57

'Don't you like any who aren't Jewish?' he asked rather sharply.

Her eyes hardened, revealing a measure of the short-tempered shrew he'd suspected was lurking in there. She answered his question with another question. 'Is there anything wrong with liking Jewish poets?'

Harold shook his head. 'Nothing at all. But what about the others? You miss a lot if you deliberately limit your view.'

'My view, if I may say so, is not at all limited.'

'But the only poems you read are by Jews. I suppose you stick to Hebrew novelists, too.'

'It would take me a lifetime,' Jessica snapped, her voice hardening to match her eyes, 'to absorb even a fraction of my cultural heritage. Why should I waste a second of that time on . . . on . . .'

'Broadening your outlook?' Harold offered.

The door opened and Mrs Legg came in bearing a tray with a bottle of sherry and two glasses. 'It occurred to me you might like . . .' She hesitated, seeing the way Jessica was glaring at Harold. 'Is something wrong?'

Harold nodded briskly. 'Just about everything, I'd say.' He made the briefest bow towards Jessica and crossed to the door. As he passed his mother he murmured, 'Don't ever do this to me again.' He strode into the hall and got his coat. His mother remained in the doorway, staring at him. He slipped on the coat and stepped close to her again. 'Tell father I'll be in touch soon. And remember – if anything like this happens again, *ever*, you'd best take a long, last look at my face.'

He left, practically sprinting along the drive to his car. As he reached it and fumbled out the keys he wondered, suddenly, what Judith would have thought. How would she react if she witnessed his mother's grisly attempts to fill the gap in his life? She would probably have laughed, he decided. It was fanciful, but comforting, to imagine that she really was laughing, somewhere, at that very moment.

6

Mrs Plunkett the laundry supervisor sidled up to Pauline. 'You know what they say,' she murmured.

'No. What?'

'In spring a young man's fancy turns to what the girls have been thinkin' about all winter.'

'Leave off.' Pauline brushed back a strand of hair and tucked it under her white cap. She was embarrassed. It always embarrassed her when other people at the laundry turned their attention to her private life. She threw the switch on the side of the big ironing machine and spread out a bed sheet in front of the rollers.

Mrs Plunkett's little button eyes twinkled. 'He's a bit of a catch, you know. Good looks, a flash motor, an' he's generous when it comes to layin' out a few quid, I'm told.'

'I just said I'd go out for a drink with him. I'm not plannin' to lead him down the aisle.'

'It's always as well to look to the future,' Mrs Plunkett chirruped. 'Findin' a shortcut out of this place would be a priority with me, if I was as young as you an' had your looks.'

Pauline clamped her mouth shut and concentrated on getting the sheet into the rollers without wrinkling it. Mrs Plunkett watched for a moment, then wandered away and vanished in the swirling steam from the other machines.

'Nosey old boot,' Pauline muttered. As usual, Mrs Plunkett had been eavesdropping. The subject of her comment was Gerry Carter, an independent supplier of enzyme cleaning agents. The laundry had switched to his product six months ago, when a demonstration had convinced the management there was more profit to be gained from the enzyme method, especially in their dry-cleaning department. Since that time Gerry, who made his own deliveries, had been to the laundry at least once a week. On his fourth or fifth visit he had begun taking an interest in Pauline.

At first she hadn't liked him. He was good-looking all right; he had an open, handsome face and really large blue eyes. His hair was always smartly styled. But he was a bit too flash for Pauline's taste and his patter always sounded as if it had been rehearsed. The first few times he spoke to her she gave him the time of day and that was all. He got no encouragement.

That morning, though, he had arrived at the laundry to find Pauline feeling vulnerable and low.

'You're lookin' a bit gloomy today, Sunshine,' Gerry had said. 'What's up?'

'Nothin'.'

'Oh yeah? It don't look like nothin' to me.'

'You're an expert, are you?'

'At removin' stains,' he said. 'An' you've got a big one, right in the middle of your cheerfulness. How's about I pick you up tonight and take you for a drink an' a few laughs?'

Pauline had found herself smiling. She felt flattered, too, at the way he seemed to focus every atom of his attention on her. When he put the invitiation to her a second time, she accepted.

'Great,' he said. 'I'll be round about half-eight.' He frowned for a moment, as if he was trying to recall something. 'It's Albert Square, right? Number forty-five?'

'How'd you know that?' Pauline demanded.

'I collect names an' addresses.' He winked and moved off. 'I'll see you tonight.'

For the rest of the day Pauline went about her work with a sense of relief. Things were changing, at long last. She had been seeing Arthur Fowler, more or less regularly, since the previous May. That very morning she had decided that ten months of him was about as much as she could take.

There was something depressingly static about Arthur. When they went out now it was the same as when they first went out. He had made no effort to develop the relationship. Pauline's own attempts had no effect. It was as if Arthur was content just to let things bowl along as they were, indefinitely; twice-a-week visits to the pub or the pictures, home again, a quick kiss on the doorstep and that was that.

'It's not that I'm lookin' for a big romance, or nothing',' Pauline explained to a friend on the way home. 'I just want to get rid of the feelin' I've got, like I've been hitched for years. That's the way we've got, Arthur an' me. We're like them couples you see in the pub. Sittin' like statues, starin' into space, never sayin' a word to each other.'

'Arthur's just a bit stodgy,' her friend said. 'He could change, with a bit of nudgin'.'

'Nudgin'? I've nudged till me elbow's black an' blue.'

And while she had been nudging, she had never been certain it was a good idea. Pauline wasn't even sure she and Arthur could have any real future together. She had learned to like a lot of things about him – but she liked lots of things about puppies and kittens, birds and butterflies. Arthur definitely did not fire her. Only her romantic dreams did that. Since none of the men who featured in those dreams – Stewart Grainger, Henry Fonda, Steve McQueen – were ever likely to know she existed, or likely to care a damn even if they did know, she reasoned it was only realistic to see if the likes of Gerry Carter could inject some real-life romance, or just fun, into her existence.

'About time I had a bit of excitement, anyway,' she said as she and her friend parted on the corner of Bridge Street. 'Arthur's idea of excitement is orderin' up another couple of drinks just before closin' time.'

That evening she took great care over her appearance. Recently, matters had reached a point where she just had a quick comb and threw on a coat when Arthur showed up at the back door. Tonight, she was determined to look as close to stunning as she could manage.

Her blonde hair, she decided, looked best brushed to the side, with the ends part-covering one eye, the way Mary Quant sometimes did hers. When it came to the make-up, she used plenty of eye-liner and the new lacquer-look lip gloss; she made the skin of her face fashionably pale with a smooth layer of foundation. After a lot of dithering, she decided to wear the yellow mini shift dress she had got for eight shillings a week from her Aunt Queenie's Littlewoods catalogue. She completed the ensemble with beige grannie-shoes and her white raincoat, which she would probably carry over her arm, since she would be travelling in a car.

'So where's Arthur takin' you tonight that's so special?' Louise wanted to know. 'Done up like a dish of fish, you are.'

'I'm not goin' out with Arthur,' Pauline said. She was hovering by the front window, anxiously watching the empty, lamplit square. It had begun to occur to her, as eight-thirty arrived, that Gerry might not show up.

'Oh. Goin' out with the girls from work, then?'

'No.'

Louise sat down on the couch, running her appraising eye over Pauline again, shaking her head. 'Must be somethin' really special to make you go to all that trouble.'

Pauline looked at her mother. 'All what trouble? I've only put on a bit of make-up an' that.' She returned her gaze to the window and saw the long blue bonnet of Gerry's car slide into view. She snatched up her coat and hurried out to the hall. 'I don't think I'll be late,' she called. 'Ta-ra.'

Louise went to the window and looked out. She saw

Gerry, in a narrow-lapelled green blazer, striped shirt and floral tie, get out of the car and swagger round the other side to open the door for Pauline.

'What the hell's she gettin' up to?' Louise murmured. 'Looks like a right wide boy, that one.'

The car was pulling away when Louise heard a tap on the kitchen door. By the time she got there Pete was coming in, carrying the baby. Pat was behind him, looking sullen as ever.

'Hello, Mum. Brought young David to see you,' Pete said.

Louise came forward, holding out her arms. 'Let's have him, then.' She took the baby and held him close. 'Hello Davie boy,' she cooed.

'We're tryin' not to call him Davie,' Pat said. Pete shot her a warning glance, which Louise didn't miss. 'We want people to use his proper name.'

Louise said nothing. She was learning to swallow Pat's corrections and contradictions. She waggled her head at the baby. He gazed back with wide, off-focus eyes. He was only two months old, a fact which puzzled Louise. If Pat had truly been pregnant when she got married, David would have been born around November or December. Louise often had to will herself not to dwell on the matter, although she couldn't help suspecting her son had been hoodwinked.

'We can't stop long,' Pete said.

'Long enough for a cup of tea, surely?'

'Well . . .' His eyes flickered towards Pat.

'We're on the way to my auntie's,' Pat said crisply. 'She's giving us supper, then we're goin' to watch her holiday slides.'

'Oh, well . . .' Louise smiled at the baby, jiggling him gently in the crook of her arm. 'Maybe you'd like to come round Saturday. For tea.'

'Yes,' Pete said, 'that'd be – '

'We're goin' out Saturday,' Pat reminded him. To

Louise she said, 'My Mum's lookin' after David so we can go to the pictures an' maybe have a drink after. I haven't seen a film in months.'

'Well, we'll arrange somethin' a bit later,' Louise said. 'How are things with you anyway, Pete? Work goin' all right?'

'Could be worse, Mum.'

Pat sniffed. 'Could be a lot better.'

Louise looked from one to the other. 'Somethin' up?'

'He's got two weeks' notice, that's what's up.' Pat drew the lapels of her coat about her neck, as if the air in the kitchen might harm her.

'I've not been happy there, anyway.'

'You don't go to work to be happy,' Pat snapped.

'Look, I wanted somethin' different, anyway. Somethin' that suited me better.'

Now Pat was openly sneering at him. 'Such as what? Lead singer with a rock an' roll group? Games organizer at Butlins? All that stuff you talk about, you'd think you were somethin' special.'

Louise was compelled to speak. 'He was special enough for you to want to marry him.'

Pat glared at Pete, as if he had said that. 'Tell you what,' she hissed, 'I'll just take David on round to Auntie Sarah's an' you can stop here for a bit of pettin'.'

'No call for that,' Louise said.

Pat took the baby from her, almost snatching him. 'No call for it, you reckon? If you ask me, he's a sight too green to leave his mum.'

Pete grasped her elbow. 'Put a bloody lid on it, Pat!'

'Don't play the big man! It might fool some, but it don't impress me!'

David began to cry.

'For God's sake,' Louise said, 'stop it, the pair of you. You're frightenin' the wits out of the baby.'

Pat turned, clutching the yelling child, and pulled open

64

the door. 'I'm off.' She shot a hard look at Pete. 'You can please yourself what you do.'

For an aching second he stood looking at his mother. She could see he wanted to stay, wanted to talk to her. 'On you go,' Louise told him as Pat disappeared into the yard.

'Mum . . .'

Louise jerked her head at the door. 'They're both your responsibility, like it or not.'

'I know, but . . .'

'But bugger all. A man sees to his responsibilities, Pete. He handles them himself.'

He nodded and turned to the door. 'Right.' He stared into the yard. 'I'll see you some time later in the week, I suppose.' He went out and closed the door.

Louise remained where she was, frowning at the darkness beyond the kitchen window, hearing the baby's cries and Pat's rasping, scolding voice tailing off along Bridge Street.

By ten o'clock Pauline was feeling light-headed. Without the drinks, she believed, she would have been a lot more bored than she already was.

They were in a plastic and chrome nightclub with swirling lights, raucous music and uncomfortable bar stools, a place where Gerry had been making some show of being well-known. It hadn't taken many minutes for Pauline to realize that he was hardly known there at all. The few people who recognized him didn't appear to like him. One man he slapped on the shoulder had looked threateningly hostile.

For the first twenty minutes Pauline felt she was enjoying herself. Everything was new to her – the discotheque atmosphere, the cocktail bar, the West-End trendies. But Gerry's relentless campaign of self-advertising soon wore through the novelty.

Throughout four, or it may have been five drinks,

Pauline had heard all about him. There was his boyhood talent on the football field, and how they had wanted him to join up as a Chelsea trainee at Stamford Bridge. His ambition, though, went well beyond that. He explained how he had made glowing successes of three businesses, then had got bored with them and sold out. On the social side, he revealed that he had squired some highly sought-after ladies around the affluent playgrounds of Europe and the Mediterranean. Coyly, he confessed that he had once been on *very* friendly terms with a lady pop singer, but he was too much of a gentleman to say who.

By now Pauline knew, beyond any doubt, that she was in the company of a typical East End windbag. Oddly, he had seemed a lot different in the laundry.

'I first had one of these on the Costa del Sol,' Gerry was saying, holding up his dry martini. 'Or was it in Crete?'

'Mile End Road, more like,' the barman muttered.

Gerry ignored him. 'Finest cocktail in the world, Pauline. An acquired taste, of course, but to the educated palate . . .' He bunched the fingertips of his free hand and kissed them. 'Superb.'

'Yeah, it looks nice,' Pauline said.

'You should try one.'

'No thanks. I'll stick with the gin an' tonic.' Her last two, in fact, had been straight tonics, but her head still felt half full of air.

Gerry slurped some of his drink and put down the glass. 'Where do you fancy goin' next?'

'Well . . .' Pauline couldn't see the evening getting any more exciting, wherever they went. The real worry was that it could get more tedious. 'I should go home soon, really . . .'

'Home? *Home*?' Gerry looked extravagantly devastated. 'At this time of night? You're not serious.'

'I've got to be up for work in the mornin'.'

'Aw, one late night won't kill you.'

She was about to get firm about it when a big man came across and stood beside Gerry's stool, eyeing him as if there was something unspeakable stuck to his face. Gerry tried to return the stare, but his eyes didn't seem to be up to it.

'Fancy seein' you here,' the man said. He had a face that was perfectly designed for scowling. 'Did you know Big Curly wanted a word with you?'

'Big Curly? No, I didn't as a matter of fact.' Gerry's voice had lost its bravura rhythm. To Pauline it sounded distinctly squeaky.

'He's been tryin' to get in touch for weeks, he says.'

'Fancy that. Well, if I see him around . . .'

'Oh you will, Gerry. He'll be in here later.'

Gerry nodded. 'Great.' As the man turned and walked away he kept on nodding, as if he had lost control of his head.

'Friend of yours?' Pauline asked him.

'Mm? Oh, him, yeah – well, more an acquaintance, you might say.' He picked up his glass and finished the martini in one gulp. 'Maybe we should go, like you said.' He was watching the entrance. 'I don't want to get involved in no borin' business chat this late at night.'

'Right,' Pauline said. 'I'll just finish my drink.'

He got off the stool and stood tapping his foot while she drained the glass. At the cloakroom, Pauline thought he might suddenly break into a run as they waited for the girl to get her coat. His agitation mounted steadily as they climbed the stairs, and when he pulled open the door he looked to right and left along the pavement before he stepped outside.

They were halfway back to Walford before Gerry began to relax again. From the corner of her eye Pauline saw him watching her, taking swift peeks as they passed under bright street lamps.

'I'll tell you something, Pauline,' he said eventually. 'I can sense when two people just sort of, you know, mesh.'

'Pardon?'

'You an' me. We get on together. In a special way. It's a thing I can tell, nearly straight away. Hadn't you noticed it?'

'In a special way? No, I hadn't noticed.'

'Oh, it's there. It's there, all right. Call it the right chemistry, good vibrations – call it what you want.'

If Pauline had been with someone she knew better, she would have called it bullshit.

'It don't happen often in a person's life,' he went on. 'Comin' across somebody that's just right for him. For her.'

At a shadowy corner he slowed the car and turned into a dark, narrow street. Another turn took them into what looked like an alley. Gerry braked, switched off the engine and killed the lights. An instant later Pauline felt his warm breath on her cheek.

'You're my kind of girl,' he told her throatily. With a shock she felt his hand land on her knee.

'Here!' she snapped, jerking it away. 'Pack it in!'

'Don't be like that.' His puckered lips put a damp circle on her cheek. Pauline turned her head. She couldn't see his face. There was only the shadowy outline of his head, the smell of Old Spice and his raspy breathing. 'Come on, lover,' he whispered urgently. 'Let go. Just let go.' This time his hand darted under her dress and clamped around her thigh.

'Chuck it, I said!' With an effort Pauline dislodged his fingers and swiftly crossed her legs. 'Get this bleedin' car started an' take me home! Right now!'

His bulk moved across her and she felt him nudge at her breast. 'Come on,' he hissed urgently. 'You know the score. Don't play hard to get . . .'

Pauline bunched her left hand and brought it up in a tight arc. It struck his ear with a crack.

'Ow!' He lurched away from her, landing back in his own seat. 'What was that all about?'

'You know what it's about! Get your mucky paws on that wheel and get this car movin'!'

For a moment he just sat there rubbing his ear. 'Listen,' he hissed. 'Do you realize I spent four quid on you?' He was suddenly on her again, grabbing her by the shoulders. 'It's a straightforward deal an' you know it. You either lie back, or walk back.'

The hatpin Pauline always carried had been in her hand for three seconds. One second later a quarter of its length was in Gerry's arm. He roared and flew backwards, banging his head on the windscreen. As he pitched forward and caught his chin on the back of his seat, Pauline opened the door and slid out of the car.

She strode to the end of the alley, buttoning her raincoat as she went. On the main street she stopped to get her bearings, then clopped off in the direction of the Walford boundary.

She had gone fifty yards when she heard Gerry's car screech out on to the main road and go roaring past her. She watched the tail lights disappear. So much for a bit of excitement, she thought. She'd be knackered by the time she got back to Albert Square.

At a corner she stopped to let a bus go past. Sitting at the back there was a young man who looked just like Arthur Fowler. He sat the same way as Arthur, too, hunched forward a little, making no show of himself, content to be allowed his space. Pauline wished, with an intensity that was almost a pain, that Arthur was with her. Until now, she hadn't realized how much she preferred the quiet, stodgy type.

7

Six weeks after he had promised to consider taking over
the private practice, Harold Legg finally told his father
what he had decided. It was at the end of one of
their fortnightly joint clinics. They were taking coffee in
Gregory's office.

'I've thought about it carefully,' Harold said. 'I considered every aspect, every pro and con. I've made a few
mercenary calculations, too. I thought ahead, to what it
could mean for me in ten or fifteen years – in private
practice I could be doing *terribly* well by the time I'm
fifty-five. But still I have to say no, Father. I can't give up
my own practice.'

One of Gregory's longer silences followed. Harold
watched him, imagining his father reluctantly laying to
rest all his hopes for the practice, one by one.

After a minute, Gregory said, 'There's no room left for
argument, then?'

'I've used every argument on myself. I even talked to
Roger Lewis about it. He spoke up very persuasively on
your behalf. But in the end the same old truth persisted.
Where I am is where I belong.'

'It makes me very sad, Harold.' Gregory put down his
cup. 'But I do understand. Your patients are fortunate to
have a doctor who shows them such powerful loyalty.'

'Father, I thought of a compromise, of sorts. I don't
know what you'll think of it . . .'

'Tell me and we'll see.'

'Well. There are eight long-term patients on your
books. At one time and another I've dealt with all of
them. There are another six, I'd say, who look like
becoming long-termers.'

Gregory nodded. The patients Harold referred to were people who were not curable. Their heart conditions would not shorten their lives, however, so long as they were regularly monitored and had their treatment adjusted from time to time.

'What I thought,' Harold said, 'was that I could go on seeing that group after you retire – one day a week, say. There's an empty room in my place at Islington that would make an ideal surgery.'

Gregory looked brighter already. 'Harold,' he said, smiling, 'that's a splendid idea. Perfectly splendid.'

'It's far from being all you wanted, but . . .'

'To be frank, it's the future of the long-term cases that has troubled me most. They've been coming to me for so long, it would be hard for them to adjust to a new face. But as you say, they know you . . .'

'And I'd be keeping my hand in, which I want to do, anyway.'

For the next ten minutes they discussed the details. Gregory grew almost excited as he made notes of case-histories to be expanded for Harold's benefit and decided on which items of equipment he could spare to establish the new surgery.

At three o'clock Harold said he had to get back for late surgery. His father walked to the front door with him and they stood outside for a minute on the steps.

'Thank you again, Harold.' Gregory patted his shoulder.

'So long as you're not totally disappointed.'

'I'll tell you the truth. I feel scarcely any disappointment at all, thanks to your compromise.' He rubbed his hands slowly. 'Now if things could be worked out as amicably and satisfactorily at home, I'd be in a state of grace, relatively speaking. But your sister. She's upsetting your mother, which means I get no peace.'

'What's Miriam been doing now?'

'It's what she plans to do. She's set her heart on going to live in Israel.'

'Lord,' Harold groaned. 'That won't please mother. Miriam's her staunchest ally. What'll she do without her?'

'I suspect, Harold, that she'd like to go to Israel, too.'

Harold frowned. 'But surely you'd never want to uproot yourself like that?'

'Not in the least. Not to go to Israel, anyway. So. There is tension.'

'Any time it gets too much for you,' Harold said, 'give me a call and we'll go out to dinner. An evening of self-indulgence works wonders for the frazzled spirit.'

'I'll probably take you up on that.' Gregory stood waving as Harold went down the steps. He remained by the door, smiling faintly, watching until his son was out of sight.

A week later Harold received a letter from his sister. In it, she informed him that in six weeks' time she and her husband would be going to Tel Aviv, where he would take up a hospital appointment. She would work for a Zionist propaganda agency. Harold was invited – though not cordially, he was sure, considering his history of conflict with Miriam – to a farewell party that would be given one week before their departure.

Harold looked up from the letter as someone tapped on the surgery door. The clock said five minutes to nine.

'Yes?'

Ethel Skinner came in and closed the door behind her. Without being invited to, she came and sat down in front of the desk.

'The shop isn't open for five minutes yet, Ethel.'

'It's urgent, Doctor. I thought I'd better come an' tell you straight away.'

Ethel never bothered to put on street clothes when she came to the surgery. She simply came down from the flat upstairs as she was. This morning she wore a flowery wrap-around apron and fluffy pink slippers.

72

'Urgent? Is something the matter with William?'

'No. But there's somethin' goin' to be wrong with Rita Loveridge, over at the caff on Bridge Street.'

'I'm not with you, Ethel.'

'I saw it, Doctor. Just now.'

Harold narrowed his eyes at her. 'Tea leaves again, is it?'

'Not exactly. I *was* lookin' at the leaves when it just came to me. Like it does, sometimes. I saw danger. An accident happenin' to Rita Loveridge.' Ethel had spells of clairvoyance, over and above her routine talents with tea leaves and palmistry. 'I thought you'd better know.'

Harold scratched his nose thoughtfully. 'It's good of you to warn me, Ethel.'

She sat blinking at him. 'Aren't you goin' to go over there?'

'Well no . . .'

'Oh but you should, it could be very serious.'

'I've a surgery due to start any minute,' Harold explained patiently. 'If an emergency crops up over at Rita's, I'm sure I'll be alerted.'

'But wouldn't it be better to go now? I mean, maybe you could stop it happenin'.'

Harold thought quickly then said, 'You can't stop what's going to happen, can you? Not if it's foreseen. I'm sure that means it's got to happen no matter what.'

Ethel looked troubled. 'Right enough,' she murmured. She stood up. 'I reckon the best thing I can do is keep an eye out over there. Then when it does happen, whenever and whatever, I can tell you double-quick.' She stood up. 'I'll go and get me coat on.'

'Good thinking, Ethel.'

As she left Harold let out a long, slow sigh. If he was ever called upon to classify Ethel's mental state, he would be hard pressed to make an accurate evaluation. She certainly wasn't mad. There were plenty of times when she made commendably sane judgements. Her fund of

73

common sense, too, was as adequate as any in the district. But Ethel wasn't entirely normal, either, given her odd way of dressing, the attacks of premonition and her activities as a fortune-teller. She also held some political and racial opinions that were so extreme they made Hitler's views sound positively liberal.

Eccentric, Harold decided, was the kindest label to tack on Ethel's personality. That settled, his mind drifted away from her and back to his sister, as he waited for the clock to tick round to nine.

'Israel,' he murmured. There would be no living with his mother, now. Miriam was her twin in matters of faith, morality and domestic management. They had been mutually reliant since Miriam was a little girl.

Even when she had left home and taken on a husband and a house of her own, Miriam was constantly in touch with Mrs Legg, advising or receiving advice, expressing opinions, consoling. The pull of the chosen land must be very strong, Harold reflected, to take his sister so far away from his mother. And in consequence, his poor father would suffer. His wife would take out her frustration and sense of loss on him. Mercilessly. Gregory Legg's retirement was not going to be a peaceful one.

Harold's hand was poised ready to hit the bell when the door was knocked again, very loudly this time.

'Come in.'

It was a young police constable. 'Sorry to disturb you, Doctor. There's been a bit of an accident over on Bridge Street. We've belled an ambulance but I thought you should have a look in the meantime.'

'Where about on Bridge Street?'

'In the café. It's a woman, she's pretty badly cut.'

Coincidence, Harold thought sternly as he hurried across the square beside the policeman. Sheer damned coincidence. He noticed Ethel ahead of them, on her way to take up her vigil by the café. She glanced over her shoulder and saw them.

74

'Somethin' wrong, Doctor?' she called.

Harold said nothing as he ploughed on past.

'It's happened, has it?'

The constable glanced at Harold. 'What'd she mean by that, Doc?'

'Nothing. She's a bit eccentric.'

They entered the café and the policeman led the way through to the back. To his surprise, Harold saw Rita Loveridge standing by the sink without a mark on her.

'She's terribly pale,' Rita said, pointing to a woman in a chair in the corner.

'What happened?' Harold asked, going across.

'She was standin' over the road there, just under the bridge, waitin' to cross, I think – '

'It didn't happen here, then?' Harold patted the woman's shoulder as he carefully unwound the tea towel from her arm. She was shivering, partly in shock.

'No. There was a lorry cornerin' a bit tight, like they're always doin', an' a bloody great chunk of scrap metal fell off. Hit her right on the arm. Cut clean through her coat, poor soul. I heard her squealin' an' brought her in here.'

The wound was deep but no artery or major veins were involved. Harold took a tension dressing from his bag and began positioning it over the injury. Ethel appeared in the doorway, craning her neck. She was about to say something as the ambulance arrived. She stepped aside to let the attendant come in.

When the woman had been despatched to hospital Harold washed his hands, picked up his bag and said goodbye to Rita Loveridge. He could see Ethel waiting for him out by the counter.

'You see?' she said as he came out.

'It wasn't Rita it happened to, Ethel.' He had no wish to hurt her feelings, or to diminish her mystical sense of herself; he was pointing out the discrepancies for his own peace of mind. 'And it didn't even happen in here.'

'Even so, Doctor.'

They left the café together and walked back towards the square. 'That's how it is, sometimes,' Ethel said. 'A bit of a jumble. But the bits are usually all there, like they was this morning. Danger, an accident, the café, Rita . . .'

It was often difficult, Harold thought, to be a rational person in a world like this. His family was being disrupted by religious fervour, and his professional objectivity was under assault from clairvoyance. He was hemmed-in by absurdity.

'We don't understand the half of what's goin' on, do we Doctor?'

'That's a fact, Ethel.'

Short of trading his stethoscope for a crystal ball, though, Harold saw no alternative but to put up with it, and try not to get too bewildered.

8

By the summer of 1966 the troubled marriage of Pete and
Pat Beale had reached a point where hostility dominated
nearly every hour they spent together. In the course of
many a silent aftermath, when abuse had been hurled,
accusations aimed and spite noisily vented, Pete admitted
to himself that their marriage had been a black and
terrible mistake.

The misery apart, he had never known such loneliness.
Nightly he lay by the side of a woman who flinched if he
touched her, even accidentally. By day he worked long
hours alone in a smelly, filthy shed, remoulding car tyres.
When he went home in the evening, he often had to run
the gauntlet of his omother-in-law's mute disdain on his
way to the cramped quarters at the top of the house.
Often he made his own tea while his wife sat frowning at
the television set, saving up her resentment until there
was enough for another row. Even the child, David, was
reluctant to have anything to do with Pete.

One overcast evening in July, as he came home weary
and dirty with the rank smell of molten rubber still
clinging to his clothes and skin, he sensed he was walking
into another bout of conflict. Like an animal, he had
learned to interpret the atmosphere.

The air in their tiny living room was dense and oppress-
ive. Pat was sitting by the open window, staring down at
the street. Her skin looked blotchy and her hair was
uncombed. She was six months pregnant and the solid
mound of her belly rested heavily on her lap.

'Where's David?' Pete asked as he hung up his jacket.

'Downstairs with Mum.' Pat turned her head slowly.
She looked at him for a second, then wrinkled one side

of her nose, drawing up the corner of her mouth. 'You stink.'

'I know. I'll wash and get changed.'

'How can you bear to go around smellin' like that?'

'I've no choice, Pat. I've got a smelly job.'

'It's horrible. It's worse than it usually is, an' that's bad enough.'

'Yeah. Right. I've got the message.' He pulled his shirt out of his trousers and began to unbutton it.

'Do that in the bedroom.'

Pete sighed softly and went through to the even tinier room where they slept. He got out of his work clothes and slipped on his cleanest trousers and shirt. There was no way of avoiding it, he thought as he paused by the mirror and ran his fingers through his hair. Pat wanted a fight.

'I thought you were goin' to have a wash,' she said when he came back into the living room.

'I'll do it later.'

'Do it now. You still stink.'

'Pat . . .'

'It might be all right for you. You're used to your smell. But I can't put up with it. It turns my stomach.'

'For cryin' out loud – it can't be that bad.'

'It's putrid!'

'You'll just have to live with it, till I get a better job.'

'Hah!'

'Pat. I'm tired. I don't want a barney tonight. OK?'

She drummed her fingers on the window ledge. 'Just tell me one thing, then. When's this better job comin' along?'

'I'm keepin' my ear to the ground. Soon as somethin' turns up, I'll grab it.'

'Like you grabbed this one?' she snapped. 'Big deal. You're always handin' out the flash talk, Pete, but it ain't worth shit at the end of the day.'

'Now listen – '

'You're goin' to hit top money soon, that's how the story goes, right? That's what you said before you took this job. You said that before I knew it, we'd have a house an' a car an' God knows how many other things. What happened? You wound up doin' a filthy horrible job even the nignogs wouldn't go near. An' what do you pick up for wages? Buttons.'

Pete glared at her. 'Will you belt up?'

'What'll you do if I don't? Lay one on me?' She waggled her head defiantly. 'That'd be just about your style an' all, hittin' a pregnant woman.'

'I'm warnin' you – '

'Stuff your warnin'!'

Pete stormed across to the sideboard and jerked open the door. He rummaged about among the packets and tins for a moment, then looked up. 'What's for me tea?'

Pat shrugged. 'Nothin', I suppose, if there's nothin' there.'

'Christ.' He looked about him helplessly. 'I brought in sliced ham an' a tin of spaghetti last night.'

'David an' me had them.'

'Don't you go out to the shops no more?'

She looked at him indignantly. 'Not feelin' as rotten as this, I don't. You wouldn't like it, bein' sick all day, feelin' like you weigh a ton . . .'

'All right, all right,' he groaned. 'I've heard it before.' He took his best shoes from under a chair and slipped them on.

'I suppose you'll go round the pub now an' have a pie an' a few pints?'

He nodded. 'Yeah. I will.'

'It's all right for some.'

Pete took his windcheater from the hook on the door. 'Come with me, if you want.'

'The smell in the pub makes me sick an' all.' She sniffed as a light breeze ruffled the curtains. 'Even the smell off the street's sickenin'.'

79

Pete stared at her, shaking his head. 'It must be hell, bein' you.'

The skin beneath her eyes tightened, signalling fresh anger. 'Yeah, it is,' she said. 'It's hell bein' cooped up all day, with nothin' decent to wear when I do go out, nothin' to look forward to at the end of the day but Mr Failure comin' in an' bringin his stink with him.'

'Shut it!' Pete barked. 'Just shut it!'

'I'll shut it when I'm good an' ready!' She stood up, her stomach jutting like a threat. 'My life's a piggin' misery Pete Beale, an' it's all down to you. I've got nothin', *nothin*' – no money, no friends left, no bloody future –'

'Snap,' Pete said. 'But at least I'm tryin' to do somethin' about it. I work hard to make things better.'

Her face twisted with disbelief. 'You what? You call that tryin' to better yourself? What you're doin' is degradin' yourself – an' me along with you. You've no pride left – you don't give a monkey's what people think when they hear what you do for a so-called livin'.'

'If I'm that much of a disgrace to you an' your bleedin' family, it might be better if I buggered off.'

'You'd like that, wouldn't you?' She was beginning to tremble. She came and stood directly between Pete and the door. 'You'd like to be out an' free with no responsibilities, havin' bags of laughs with your mates . . .'

'Yeah, I would!'

'You're a rotten selfish bastard!'

'An' you're a miserable sod. There's nothin' I can do to please you. Nothin' I do is right. Even if it is right you'll make it look wrong. While you're talkin' about the lousy life you've got, just bear in mind it ain't roses for me, neither. I wish to Christ I'd never laid eyes on you.'

'Same here!'

Suddenly, the accumulated pressures of conflict, misery and frustration seemed to jar a vital switch in Pete. Now he was angrier than she was, angry enough to put up with no more. He stamped through to the bedroom and began throwing his clothes into a plastic holdall.

Pat came and stood in the doorway, glaring at him. 'What do you think you're doin'?'

'What does it look like? I'm pissin' off.'

'You do an' I'll have the law on you!'

He fished under the bed and pulled out a pair of sandals. 'There's no law says a man can't walk out on his wife. Especially if she's a naggin', whinin', evil-tempered cow like you.' He crammed some more clothes into the bag and pulled the zipper shut. 'I've had it, Pat. I'm not takin' any more slaggin' off you.'

'So you're runnin' back to your mum, are you?' The contempt in Pat's voice didn't conceal her sudden anxiety.

'I don't know where I'm goin'.' He picked up the bag and pushed out past her. 'I'll see to your money every week, don't worry about that.' He pulled open the door.

'You come back here!'

He went out without glancing at her. As the door shut Pat let out a sharp, angry whine. 'Pete!' she howled. 'Come back here! *Pete!*'

He was nearly at Bridge Street before the enormity of it hit him. He had walked out. He had left her. The daydream was a reality that fizzed in him. Most potent of all was the understanding that he would never have to go home to Pat again.

In the cool air under the railway bridge he stopped and put down the bag. He leaned his shoulders on the wall and gazed up at the girders, taking it all in again.

For an uneasy minute he began to feel cut off, rather than free. There was still a wistful memory of Pat that none of her nagging and no amount of abuse had wiped out. He felt an abrupt pang of sadness as he realized he had put that girl behind him. And there was little David too – a surly kid, really, but his son all the same.

The sense of liberation flooded back, though, as he made himself face the unromantic truth. Pat had become

81

a tyrant, a full-weight bitch who had sealed her old self off and had even turned his child against him. That was the situation he had walked out on.

She was pregnant, of course, and leaving her in that condition would get him the worst kind of reputation in the district. But Pete could feel no guilt on that score. Pat was pregnant as the result of one rare act of sub-mission, after months of abstinence. He remembered how she had lain there, motionless, her face a stiff mask of loathing in the dim light. After that, he hadn't even contemplated touching her again.

He picked up the holdall and walked off along Bridge Street towards the Queen Victoria. A couple of drinks, he decided, would help him to make his plans. They might even supply some of the courage he would need to tell his mother what he had done.

Den Watts waved from a corner table as Pete walked into the bar, then promptly returned his attention to Angie Shaw, who had condescended to come out and have a drink with him.

'Right then,' he said, looking at her empty glass. She had finished the first drink in less than three minutes. 'Can I get you somethin' else? Excited, for instance?'

'The same again will be fine, ta.'

Den went to the bar and waited while the part-time girl served Pete. As she came towards him he switched on his smile.

'Pint of bitter, love, an' a gin an' tonic.'

At sixteen Den had the statue and bearing of a man in his twenties, which he often pretended to be. He leaned closer as the girl put the beer glass under the pump.

'What the difference between a man's plonker an' a chicken leg?' Since the time his voice broke properly he had specialized in throaty gags whenever a girl got within earshot.

She giggled. 'I don't know.'

He winked. 'Fancy comin' on a picnic?'

She was still laughing as he returned to the table with the drinks. As he sat down Angie watched him carefully, measuring his self-assurance. During the past two years they had met often, but this was the first time they had gone out together. He had changed a lot, Angie decided.

'Old Pete looks a bit forlorn, don't he?' Den said.

'Worn down's how he looks, if you ask me.'

'Yeah. I've heard it hasn't been goin' too well with him an' Pat.'

Angie swirled her drink. 'It's not surprisin', really. They got hitched too young.'

For a moment Den appraised her in silence, just as she had been inspecting him. He took in the compact little figure, the lively wide eyes, her mobile features and the tight economy of her movements. If anything, he was more excited by her now than he had been two years ago.

'It's not somethin' you'll ever do, is it Angie?'

'What?'

'Get married too young.'

She looked at him candidly, her eyes working electric magic on him, making him feel his heartbeat. 'I don't know that I'll get married at all. If I do, he'll have to be somethin' really special.'

'But you'd miss a lot, not gettin' married.'

'Such as?'

'Well . . .' There was a risk of toppling his image, Den realized. If he confessed to a belief in abiding tenderness and people growing old together, she might think he was a twerp. 'Husbands and wives, two people who really know each other, for years that is . . . They get somethin' special out of it.'

'Two people who live together without gettin' married get just as much, without the ties.'

'Would you do that? Live with a bloke?' Instantly, Den was picturing himself set up with her.

'The bloke I go out with right now, he's suggested it a couple of times.'

The information left Den with an odd sensation, like a ringing in his ears that he couldn't actually hear. 'You've got a steady?'

'Well.' Angie shrugged and began to look coy. 'We see a lot of each other, if you know what I mean.'

Den's face felt hot. He hoped he wasn't blushing. He'd never even dreamed there was another man. And as for what she was hinting at . . . It dawned on him how much more sure of himself he had felt when he talked to the barmaid.

'I haven't made up my mind about it,' Angie said. 'He's nice, but I'm not sure I could live with him.'

It was depressing for Den, the way people went on in private, but rarely showed any signs or said much about it in public. He never knew who was having a really eye-popping time on the side. Maybe it was best to assume everybody was. Everybody but him. The thought so distracted him that he didn't notice Pete drain his glass and walk out.

'This bloke you're seein',' he ventured. 'Don't he mind you goin' out with somebody else?'

'I never tell him. He never asks. If he sees other girls he doesn't tell me. It's a good arrangement. I think it'd have to change a bit, though, if we started livin' together.'

'Yeah,' Den said absently. For three years he had been hanging around girls who went to bed by eleven and never stayed out past ten. Three years of frustration, of being slapped and warned to keep his hands to himself. Any headway he made – and it was small-time stuff – had been achieved only after massive, prolonged effort and the outlay of considerable sums of cash in pubs and coffee bars.

Now, blindingly, he realized that the girl he fancied more than any of them was probably the kind to whom sex was an everyday indulgence, like eating and having a drink.

'Have you got a place of your own?' Angie asked him.

'Me? No, not at the moment.'

'Pity.'

More than a pity, he thought. A tragedy, nothing less. What might she have suggested if he did have a pad? How much was he going to miss?

'I could be gettin' a place soon,' he said quickly, hoping fervently that it might be possible, though he had no idea how. 'I've got a couple of feelers out . . .'

'Feelers? Ooh, nice,' Angie said, giggling.

This time, Den knew he was blushing.

'You've done *what*?' Louise yelped. She was glaring at Pete with such menace that he was sure she was going to hit him.

'I've had enough, Mum. I couldn't take any more of it.'

'Tough cheese! You made your bed, so you've got to lie on it!'

Pete shifted his feet, seeing his chapfallen reflection in the kitchen mirror. 'If you only knew the half of it . . .'

'I don't want to know any of it. It's no business of mine. You had your warnin's before you went into it, but you went ahead anyway. So. Now you're in, you bloody well stay in. Pick up that bag an' get back home. Now!'

'I'm not goin' back,' he said stubbornly.

'You listen to me. That's your family you're on about, in case you've forgot. They're your responsibility. You've got another kiddie on the way, an' all. What kind of man are you at all? What d'you think your Dad would say?' Louise extended an arm in the direction of the Harris's house. 'I don't want to hear no more bubblin' about what a hard life you've got. Get back there this instant and sort yourself out.'

Pete picked up the bag and went to the door.

'Now you're goin' back, aren't you? Tell me you are.'

'I can't tell you that, Mum.'

He opened the door and went out. A moment later Louise heard the yard door close. She felt something like a pain growing in her, dull and heavy. A little moan escaped her. In the nine years since Albert had died, there had been cause to miss him almost every day. She was missing him now. Terribly.

9

Leaving the sumptuous Clayton Club in the centre of Mayfair, Harold Legg was surprised at how many people he recognized. It had been the same at lunch; there seemed to be old acquaintances all over the dining room. A lot of doctors were members here, he knew that, but he had always assumed he was a lot humbler in calibre than the medical men who belonged to places like that.

At the desk the hall porter brought him his coat. 'I hope you had a pleasant lunch, sir.'

'Oh indeed I had.' Harold let the man help him into the coat. 'It wouldn't take many more like that to spoil me.' He slipped the porter a half-crown and made his way across the broad, echoing hall.

There were more nods of recognition from a group standing near the door. Two of them were doctors who worked part-time at the King George VI Hospital in Walford, as Harold now did one day a week. Another ran a psychiatric counselling group where Harold had referred a couple of his patients. He even spotted Mike Phillips, who had been a student in the same year as himself at Bart's. Phillips, bald now and wearing pebble-thick spectacles, broke away from the group and came across as Harold reached the wide entrance door.

'Harold, it's good to see you. How are you, old chap?'

'I'm fine. Prospering, even, within decent limits. What are you doing with yourself nowadays? The last I heard, you'd gone into general surgery.'

'Still in the field,' Phillips said, nodding. In his youth he had been rather stuffy and pompous, a creature with few social graces and a monumental, deeply boring obsession with the war. Now he looked more relaxed;

there was even a hint of gentle cynicism in his smile. 'I've reached the curious stage in my career where I've had so much experience, I don't believe I know much at all any longer. My certainties have flown out of the window and I'm beset with doubts. But I'm told that happens a lot in this business.'

'Yes, and it's not a bad thing in a surgeon,' Harold assured him.

'What brings you here, anyway? Are you a member?'

Harold shook his head. 'Lunch with Roger Lewis. He's still up there, jawing with some bigwig Biochemist and killing what's left of the wine.'

'He's done well for himself, old Lewis. Definitely heading for the Honours List bracket.' Phillips smiled again. 'How about you? Still out at Walford?'

'Still the modest GP,' Harold said.

Phillips' eyes wavered momentarily behind his thick glasses. 'Goodness me,' he breathed. 'One's sense of time. It's so odd. It was ages ago, wasn't it, yet I'm not conscious of very much having happened in the space between your wedding day and now. Not when I picture the time, that party . . .'

'I get the same feeling, Mike.' Phillips had been one of the guests, invited because Harold felt sorry for the isolated, friendless young man.

'You never married again, did you Harold?'

'No.'

'I never got married at all. Who'd have me, eh?' Somebody called to Phillips as his group began moving towards the stairs. 'Must go, old chap. It's been grand seeing you.'

They shook hands warmly and before Harold left he made a promise to stay in touch.

Out on the street he turned up his collar against the sharpening October wind. He had an hour and a half before late surgery. There would be time to straighten out some of his paper work. He decided to take a taxi back to Albert Square, rather than use the Underground as he had earlier. He waved down a cab, amusing himself with the thought that a single visit to the Clayton had already given him a hankering for the better things.

In the cab he sat back comfortably, deciding that the day's events had pleased him. It was always a pleasure, of course, to meet up with Roger Lewis. Harold had had misgivings about meeting him in the Clayton. He would rather have gone to a pub or a modest restaurant. As it turned out, he found the atmosphere of the club very pleasant, almost soothing. If he was ever invited again, he would accept without a second's hesitation. If he was invited to join, he wasn't sure what he would do.

Seeing Mike Phillips had been a bonus. They had never been real friends, but Mike conjured memories of the happiest times in Harold's life – his student days and those two brief years with Judith. There had been no such joy in him before those days, or since. He thought of Judith and felt a sharper-than-usual pang. Too much wine, he told himself gruffly.

'Sad business that,' the driver said through his open partition. The remark startled Harold. It was as if the man had tuned in to his thoughts.

'Sorry?'

The driver jerked his thumb at a billboard by the traffic lights.

144 DEAD AT ABERFAN

'Terrible,' Harold said.

'All them futures wiped out, eh?'

'Terrible,' Harold said again. The first news had come the previous afternoon. A mountain of slag had descended without warning on a Welsh mining village. In minutes it engulfed the school and nearby houses. Of the dead, 116 were children. It was the kind of thing, Harold reflected, to make you shake a fist at God, if you had any certainty he was there.

At the surgery he made a pot of coffee then settled to clearing the backlog of mail and advertising that filled a drawer of the desk. He had discarded half of the leaflets and a similar proportion of letters when he was distracted by shouting out in the square. It was loud enough to be distinguishable from the cries of the market traders on Bridge Street.

He went to the window and listened, unable to see much beyond the top of the steps. The voices were women's, two of them, and he was sure one belonged to Louise Beale. Whatever was going on, they were angry.

Harold went back to his desk. He would regard the matter as none of his business, unless it reached the point where one of the parties needed his professional attention. He smiled as he sat down and picked up another letter. It was a far cry from the elegance and civilized charm of Mayfair and the Clayton Club to the boisterous, occasionally anarchic atmosphere of Walford. On balance, though, he had no doubt which he would opt for, if he were forced to choose.

The telephone rang. Harold snatched up the receiver.

'Dr Legg speaking.'

He listened, frowning at the jumbled, squeaking torrent from the other end.

'Mother,' he said, 'Mother, listen to me – speak more slowly, I can't make out a word you're saying.' The line went silent for a moment, then his mother spoke again, slowly as he had asked. Harold listened carefully. The colour began to drain from his face.

'When?'

He drew a hand across his forehead and pressed the receiver closer to his ear. His mother was beginning to babble again.

'Do nothing,' Harold said when she had finished. 'I'll be there as soon as I can.'

He put down the 'phone and sat staring at the wall opposite. Shock had left very little room in him for feeling. One impulse was surfacing, though. As the seconds passed it was being fired, steadily, by an illogical spark of anger. For the second time that day, Harold wanted to rebuke a God he scarcely believed in.

He picked up the telephone again, dialled slowly and waited. After a few seconds a woman with a Polish accent answered.

'Hello? Dr Rosewicz? This is Harold Legg.'

As he moistened his lips the small, hot anger in him was abruptly washed aside. Delayed sorrow flooded over him. He took a deep, steadying breath before he explained why he had called.

'I wonder if you could cover the surgery for me this afternoon? It's very short notice, I know. But I've just learned that my father has died suddenly.'

He nodded at the received a couple of times, murmured his thanks and put it down. With trembling hands he covered his eyes and sank back in the chair.

Out in the square, Louise was backing along the short path in front of her house, trying to get the dispute off the street and indoors where it belonged. But Lydia Harris, Pat's mother, wanted it out in the open.

'It's as much your responsibility as his!' she yelled. 'He's your flamin' son! All you're doin' is shieldin' him!'

'I'm doin' sod all of the sort!' Louise retorted. 'Now you come in here an' we can talk this over like grown-up women, instead of slangin' each other out here like brawlin' kids.'

'Oh. It's embarrassin' you, is it?' Lydia folded her arms and looked up and down the Square. 'I suppose you don't want your neighbours knowin' about it.' She jutted her chin as she took a step nearer Louise. 'Well they *should* know! They should be told about that layabout son of yours hidin' behind his mum's skirts while the wife he abandoned is in hospital havin' his kid! A right bloody charmer he is, an' no mistake!'

People were listening, out in the square and behind window curtains. Louise took another step nearer the door. 'I'll say this one more time. Come into the house. If you put me in the picture I'll see the right thing's done. But I'll not argue about it out here.'

The promise of restitution seemed to take some of the anger from Lydia. She glanced about the square again and took a step inside the gate. 'I'm not goin' to be fobbed off, mind,' she warned.

'Nobody's talkin' about fobbin' nobody off. Come in.' Louise held the door wide. 'We'll get this sorted out, one way or another.'

In the kitchen Lydia huffily accepted a cup of tea. The two women sat down and faced each other.

'Right,' Louise said, 'I'll give you my side of it, so's you get it straight. Pete ain't here. I've not laid eyes on him since the summer.'

'Where the hell is he, then?'

'I told your Pat when she was round before. He's livin' rough.'

'I don't reckon she believed that.'

'It's true, as far as we know. His brothers have looked for him, I've hunted for him, but all we've got, so far, is a rumour that he's dossin'. I've no idea where. I think he keeps on the move.'

'Can't the police find him?'

Louise stared. 'Police? We're not draggin' them into it, thanks very much. He's not done nothin' the law can touch him for, anyway.'

Lydia sucked her teeth. 'Maybe not this time.'

'We're talkin' about Pat an' him,' Louise reminded her sharply. 'Nothin' else.'

'It should be a police matter. Walkin' out on a girl with one kid an' another on the way.'

Louise sighed. 'The worry of it's made me sick, I'll tell you that. When I saw him last I told him to get back an'

92

sort out his life. I don't hold with a man leavin' his family any more than you do.'

'Leavin'_them's bad enough, but there hasn't been a penny for their support since the last few measly quid he sent in August.' Lydia put down her tea cup and folded her arms. 'So where does that take us? You was on about the right thing gettin' done, but I don't see how anybody can do anythin' if the sod's took off.'

'What's happenin' with Pat?'

'It's about her I came to tell you.'

Bad as she felt, that almost made Louise laugh. She had been shaking the doormat when Lydia came round the corner. She had started screeching abuse the instant she saw Louise.

'She's not had the baby yet?'

'She's in the hospital. Has been since last night. She might have had it by now for all I know. She was well into labour an hour ago.'

'Right.' Louise stood up and left the kitchen. She returned a minute later with a folded wad of banknotes. She held it out to Lydia.

'What's that?'

'There's ninety pound there. I'll make sure she gets more. This should see to her needs for the time bein'.'

Lydia showed only the barest token of resistance to the offer. She looked at the money again, looked at Louise, then took it and stuffed it into her coat pocket.

'You'll let me know what she has, will you?' Louise said.

'I'll send word, yes.' Lydia stood up, no longer able to meet Louise's eyes. 'I'm sorry about all that out there. I was just that flamin' mad . . .'

'Yeah, well, I reckon you'd good enough cause.'

Lydia left by the back door. As she stepped outside Louise said, 'I'll find out where our Pete is. Somehow. When I do, I'll see he does the right thing by Pat an' the

93

kids.' Watching the yard gate swing shut she muttered, 'Either that, or I'll break his bloody back tryin'.'

At that moment Pete was less than half a mile away, in the small terrace house occupied by his brother Ronnie and his wife Gail. He had been living there for three weeks, although no one outside of the house had been told.

He was in the lounge, helping Gail sort out the monthly accounts from the fruit and vegetable suppliers and simultaneously talking about the mess he had made of the past few months. Gail, like Ronnie, was a quiet and undemonstrative person. Apart from being a loyal wife and fastidious housekeeper she had a talent, Pete had recently learned, for cutting directly through a problem to get to the underlying solution.

Pete's problem, Ronnie had decided, was theirs. He had taken in his brother one night when Pete had presented himself on the doorstep at the height of a thunderstorm. He had been unshaven, filthy, soaked and thoroughly despondent.

'I still can't get over how low I'd sunk,' he said now, passing a bundle of date-sorted bills across the table. 'I never reckoned I could turn into a tramp. But that's what I was, Gail. A hobo. I didn't want to do nothin' but scuff around, bummin' a bite here, a couple of bob there . . .'

'Well, you don't have to any more.' Gail squared the pile of paper in front of her and sat back. 'Your brother an' me are determined nothin' like that'll happen again.'

After she had given Pete a few days to regain some of his spirit and self-confidence, Gail had put his whole problem to him clearly, almost in a nutshell. He had taken the wrong road, she said; what he had to do was to go back to the fork and take the right one.

His marriage to Pat had been the start of all his woes. He needed no convincing of that. What he did need was a formula for setting himself right. Soon, Ronnie had promised, he would have a job. It was nothing glamorous – he would be loading and unloading pallets and trucks at a vegetable distributor's yard. But there would be a steady wage and a place to live until he had accumulated enough to move into a flat, or at least a bedsit of his own.

After Pete had searched his conscience and reviewed his feelings carefully, under Gail's astute supervision, he had decided there was no way in the world he could make himself go back to Pat. Accordingly, Gail promptly obtained him the necessary information on how to get a divorce. As soon as he was in a fit position he would set that ball rolling. He would untie the knot that had hobbled him for two years.

'All you have to bear in mind,' Gail said now, 'is that you've a financial duty that you can't shirk. And it'll have to come first in all your reckonin'. It's a penalty, I suppose, but you earned it.'

'I know. I'll do everythin' just like you an' Ronnie told me.' He smiled at Gail, shaking his head slowly. 'I've been a prize prawn, eh?'

Gail nodded. 'The prizest I've ever come across. But you're family, so we've got to do somethin' about sortin' you out.'

He had never known she could be so warm, so support-ive. To the rest of the family, Gail was the nice girl Ronnie was married to, full stop.

'By the way,' she said, pushing the papers into the cardboard wallet, 'there's goin' to be a big bonus for you, if you get yourself back in shape.'

'What?'

'I'm not sayin'. It's enough for now that you know about it. Knowin' what it is comes later, when you've earned a couple of stars for good behaviour.'

Pete grinned. He was beginning to feel like the man who fell in the sewer and came out covered in rose petals. He watched Gail put away the paperwork. He recalled there were some people around the market who thought

Ronnie Beale tended to look a bit smug and self-satisfied at times. It wasn't to be wondered at, Pete thought. With a wife like Gail, he probably spent the best part of the day treading air.

'Whose idea was the bonus?' he asked.

'Ronnie's and mine. It's something we both agreed on.' She looked across at Pete. 'Together's the best way to do things and make decisions. I've always thought so, anyway.'

Now why, Pete asked himself, hadn't he at least tried to marry a girl like that?

10

In keeping with Harold Legg's persistent sense of speeding time, 1967 came and went in a flurry of events that seemed, in retrospect, too numerous to have been packed into one fleeting year.

War, like everything else, appeared to take less time nowadays. In 1967 Israel did battle with the combined might of Egypt, Jordan, Syria and Iraq and defeated them in only six days.

Medicine showed signs of leaping forward instead of inching its way along, as it had before; in Africa, a surgeon called Christiaan Barnard replaced a patient's diseased heart with a healthy one taken from an accident victim.

There were swift advances and radical changes in music, cinema, theatre, art and architecture. In that year people began examining their relationships and identities in the dazzling light of new, liberated ideas. Outspokenness became a trend, though not always laudable. Bigotry and intolerance became as vocal as pacifism and the cries for universal brotherhood. In Britain's immigrant communities an atmosphere of uneasiness, even fear, grew rapidly as the speeches of Mr Enoch Powell began to make racism respectable.

In Albert Square the winter of 1967 saw off two elderly residents, both in their eighties, both from underheated houses. At number forty-five Louise Beale began to feel there might, after all, be some hope of peace in her life. Pete had a job and lived in a place of his own. He made regular maintenance payments to his wife and two sons, though to Louise's regret he still refused to consider repairing the marriage. Pauline had settled into a steady relationship with Arthur Fowler – Louise called it hum-drum, though Pauline seemed happy enough – and the oldest child Dora, now 30, had finally announced that she would probably get married some time early in 1968.

Harold Legg, whose mother and sister were both now in Israel, had begun seeing his late father's long-term patients one afternoon a week at his flat in Islington. On the 31st of December, a few minutes after he had seen the final patient of the day at the Islington surgery, Harold had a telephone call from Alf Barrett at the Queen Victoria. Alf had called to invite Harold to the pub's New Year's Eve party.

'You didn't show up last year, Doc, so this year we're remindin' you on the day.'

Harold was flustered. He would have liked more time to dream up an excuse. He stood in his small lounge, gazing across at the picture of Judith on the mantelpiece.

'Well, that's good of you, Alf. But I'm afraid I'll be tied up . . .'

'Aw come on, Doc. It's New Year, it's special. The party ain't the same unless we're all here.'

'Well I've made other arrangements, you see . . .'

'Now are you sure it's nothin' you can't put off till later?' Alf persisted.

Harold thought for a moment. His plan was the same every year. He would spend the evening alone, reading and listening to music, then at midnight he would pour himself a glass of malt whisky and spend a few silent minutes thinking of Judith. He had been doing that since the year she died. It was a very private, special ritual, the closest he ever came to religious observance. During the past year, however, he had read something that stuck in his mind. It was from an essay on bereavement, written by a French philosopher. The medical metaphor in the quotation made it easy to recall:

"The loss of the loved one creates a wound which heals only if it is left to do so. To pick at the injury – that is, to regularly dwell upon the loss, is to prolong the healing and perhaps leave an ugly scar."

After reading that, Harold had wondered about his annual ceremony of silent remembrance. He had to confess, now, that it had never brought him great peace; on the contrary, it usually upset him. Judith was best remembered, perhaps, at odd times of day, and fleetingly. That way, no great sadness resulted.

'Are you still there, Doc?'

'Yes. I've just been thinking . . .'

'So what's the verdict?'

'I'll come along tonight,' Harold said.

'Marvellous. You won't regret it.'

By eleven-thirty both bars of the Queen Victoria were crammed. Laughing, shouting heads bobbed and weaved, avoiding raised elbows and trying to keep sight of who they were communicating with. Smoke blued the air and a cocktail of alcoholic fumes made it heavy and earthily sensual. A record player set up behind the bar blared raucous music through two big speakers, but the noise of the customers was so intense that only the thud-thudding bass rhythm penetrated.

Den Watts stood with his back to the wall. He stared through weaving bodies towards the bar, where Angie Shaw was leaning. Angie wasn't aware of him. She was with her current young man. Den had missed his chance there, he was certain. She had packed in with the other man and taken up with this one, without even considering Den for the substitute. That was because he had blown it, he thought bitterly. One feverish evening at a disco he had been given his opportunity to prove himself with her, but his nerve had run out on him. Now he was on the outside. Just an onlooker. A lemon.

'Seen a ghost, Den?'

It was Kenny Beale. He had a tight grip on a pint and a hold just as tight on a frizzy blonde who looked as if her eyes were melting.

'Just dreamin',' Den said lamely.

'With this lot goin' on? You must be smokin' somethin' stronger than Benson and Hedges these days.' He jerked his arm, shaking the girl as if she were a life-size doll he had found. 'This is Chrissie, by the way. Chrissie, meet Den.'

Den nodded. The girl frowned, trying to comprehend what she had been told.

'She's a bit pissed,' Kenny explained. He ran an eye over Den's natty wide-lapelled jacket, his bell-bottom trousers and dome-capped shoes. 'You're lookin' a bit sharp, my son. What you got lined up for afters?'

Den forced a lopsided, knowing grin and went into his routine. 'Italian piece,' he said confidentially. 'She's workin' right now, down at her uncle's restaurant. I'm seein' her later. At her pad.' A brisk wink. 'Them continentals – dear oh dear. They spoil a bloke for anythin' else.'

Kenny dug him painfully in the ribs. 'Dirty devil. See an' take it easy with the pop, then. Don't want the drop ruinin' your act, do you?'

'No sweat. I've got a lillipop stick an' two rubber bands on me, just in case.'

Kenny wandered off, laughing, dragging his girlfriend with him. Den returned his attention to Angie. He felt a terrible, swelling ache in his stomach as he noticed that her boyfriend had his hand splayed comfortably across her backside. Den gulped some beer, but he could hardly swallow it.

In the other bar Reg Cox had found a pound note on the floor and had nearly been trampled picking it up. Pete Beale and his mother were hemmed in at a corner table, watching Reg's efforts to fight his way to the bar. Beside Louise, Ethel and William Cox were making a tuneless, down-tempo mess of "I Remember You".

'If Frank Ifield was dead he'd be turnin' in his grave,' Pete remarked.

'Oh leave them,' Louise muttered. 'They're happy. Ethel loves her New-Year's sing-song. Just you wait. By the time the bells have rung she'll be on the real old wartime stuff. She still plays her Vera Lynn records, you know.'

Pete lifted his mother's glass and his own. 'Same again?'

'That's right, love. Hang on.' She got out her purse.

'My treat,' Pete said. 'I told you that.'

'Now are you sure?' Louise frowned at him. 'You can't go squanderin' your money . . .'

'I'm not squanderin' nothin'. I've saved up.'

He began pushing his way through the press of bodies, noticing that for every smile he got, he picked up two or three black looks. He was quite used to that by now. Somebody dropped his glass and the crowd around him moved back, causing a tidal shift that carried Pete towards the wall. He found himself almost nose-to-nose with Dr Legg.

'All right, Pete?'

'Yes thanks, Doctor.'

'Quite a party.'

Pete nodded, leaning into the throng again. 'Pretty good,' he grunted. 'The only trouble is, you get a bit happy on one drink then you sober up tryin' to get the next one in.'

Harold laughed, wished Pete luck and returned to his conversation with Norman Block. Norman was a local schoolteacher, middle-aged, responsible, single and terribly neurotic. He had been quizzing Harold on the subject of sudden death. Norman had a dread of catching anything that would snatch him out of life before he had made his preparations for departure.

'There's definitely a lot of disease that can be avoided,' Harold said, 'but nature often springs nasty surprises that have nothing to do with disease.'

Norman's eyebrows moved closer together in a careful frown. 'Often, you say?'

Harold nodded, waiting for a particularly loud bout of cheering to die down. 'Take my own father,' he said at last. 'Sound as a bell, or so he appeared. He took exercise, was careful with his diet, never smoked and drank only in moderation. I checked his cardiovascular system regularly. He had the heart and blood pressure of a fit man of forty. I assure you, he was the very picture of health. Then one day he just fell down dead.'

'What did it?' Norman asked gravely.

'Cerebral haemorrhage. No advance signs, no warning of any kind. A little tear in the wall of a blood vessel, no bigger than a pinprick. That's all it took.'

'Good heavens.'

Harold noted the gravity of Norman's expression and decided to balance the picture with some hope. 'On the other hand,' he said, 'you can have tissues as thin as rice paper and still live to be a hundred. The great thing, I think, is not to worry. My father *was* rather inclined to fret about things. I believe worry and tension can do as much harm as all the diseases put together.'

Norman nodded and took a tension-dispelling gulp from his whisky glass.

Pete, meanwhile, had reached the bar and was trying to catch the eye of Alf or one of his assistants. Glasses were being waggled all along the bar, like the gaping beaks of hungry fledglings. As Pete set his elbows on the burnished oak and prepared himself for a long wait, he realized that a girl in the corner was staring at him. As he stared back she smiled.

'What'll it be, Pete?'

'Ah. Alf. Great. A pint of best an' a Guinness, please.'

He looked at her again while Alf got the drinks. She was still there, still staring. Still smiling, too. He wondered if he should smile back at her. She was attractive and carefully made-up, with silky, honey-coloured hair. It began to dawn on him that he knew her.

'There you go,' Alf said, putting down the Guinness beside the pint.

Pete paid him, picked up the drinks and looked across at the girl again. It clicked. She was Kathy Hills. They had been at school together. The change in her was very impressive. He gave her a smile, then turned and pushed his way back to the table. By the time he got there Pauline and Arthur had come in and joined his mother. Pete handed Louise her glass.

'I won't be a tick,' he said. 'Just spotted somebody I know.'

His mother nodded absently without breaking her conversation with Pauline. Pete began ploughing across the room again, clutching his drink.

'Well, hello,' he said, easing in beside Kathy. 'It was a minute before I recognized you.'

Her smile was wider now, brighter. 'How have you been?' she asked.

'Oh, up an' down. But life's a bit that way for everybody, I suppose.'

'Swings an' roundabouts,' Kathy said. 'You're lookin' well, anyway.'

'So are you.' He looked at the people huddled on either side. 'Here with somebody, are you?'

'No. On me own.'

'Free an' easy, eh?'

'Somethin' like that.'

Pete glanced back at the table. His mother was singing along with Ethel now. Pauline and Arthur were occupied with each other. So far as he could tell, nobody was keeping an eye on him, as they had all been doing lately. He suddenly felt like a lad again, out on his own, having a pint and chatting to a girl. It was a good feeling, better than he had remembered. He turned back to Kathy.

'Can I get you a drink?'

'Thanks very much.'

That smile, Pete thought, was really doing things to

him. *For* him. If he played his cards right, this could be a New Year's Eve to remember.

At ten seconds to midnight, loud shushing and cries of 'Order!' from the landlord and his staff laid a hush on the revellers. Everyone waited as Alf raised his watch and turned up the volume on his transistor radio.

'Five!' he yelled. 'Four! Three! Two! One!'

Big Ben rang out and a collective cheer exploded. Neighbour hugged neighbour, strangers shook hands, pals slapped backs. Groups joined hands and sang Auld Lang Syne. Happy-New-Years were noisily, here and there tearfully, exchanged and drink began to flow again from the pumps and optics.

Den Watts, trying to look and sound as jovial as the rest, suddenly found himself being spun from behind. He felt two small hands land firmly on his shoulders. When he looked down he saw Angie Shaw gazing up at him.

'Give us a kiss, then!' she yelled above the noise.

He blinked at her, then ducked forward and did as he was told. The energetic, probing little tongue forced its way past his teeth and scoured his palate for a long, blissful, unbelievable second. Then he was separate from her again, staring.

'Happy New Year, Den.'

'Happy new Year, Angie.' He looked around quickly. 'Where's your bloke?'

She wrinkled her nose. 'Went home in a huff.'

'What for?'

'I told him I'd gone off him.' Her hands crept along Den's shoulders and clasped at the back of his neck. 'Well, what are you waitin' for?'

Surprise and pleasure had filled his despondent vacuum with a bang. He felt dizzy. 'Sorry?'

'Give me another kiss, dopey.'

Throughout the pub the beat and thrum of talk, music and laughter set up a rhythm that revived even the drunkest merrymakers. Louise, Pauline, Ethel, William and Arthur had taken to the floor to give an impromptu demonstration of the Hokey-Kokey, pulling in anyone handy to swell their numbers.

By the door, Reg Cox stood with his walking stick at the ready, prepared to crack any shin that came too near his own. Only the doctor and a couple of sightless drunks had so far wished Reg a happy New Year, but he didn't really mind; in the hubbub that erupted at midnight, he had managed to snatch somebody's double whisky. He took a deep, prodigal gulp from the glass, staring balefully at the happy people around him.

In the farthest corner Pete Beale was relishing an intense, elevating, glowing sensation that started at the crown of his head and enveloped every inch of him. He wouldn't have been surprised to look down and discover it was visible. For the first time in years he was enjoying himself in the company of a girl, feeling all the tricky, shivery, shifting sensations a new encounter brings. He had forgotten what it was like.

'Well,' he said, 'if the start of the year's anythin' to go on, it's goin' to be a cracker.'

At midnight he had given Kathy one chaste kiss. The impact on him was devastating – the more so because he suspected it might come under the heading of adultery. Now he considered giving her another, then decided not to trifle with his luck. Instead, he asked her if she had made a New Year's resolution.

'Yeah, I have.'

'What is it?'

'It's bad luck to tell,' Kathy said. 'But I *can* say it's to do with tryin' hard. Very hard.'

'That's funny. So's mine.'

They gazed at each other, then Pete began to grin. A moment later Kathy did, too.

11

It was the third week in January and it was snowing. Louise stood by the window, watching the big flakes slant across the square and settle, each taking longer to melt than the one before. It was going to lie, she thought dismally. She hated it when the snow stayed. There was always a deathly chill around her ankles at those times and it brought back the aches in her joints. She was turning away from the window when she saw a dark red car draw up at the gate.

A man got out who reminded Louise of the one who had once called for Pauline. He had a spivvy look, a camel-coated, paisley-scarved, brown hatted veneer that didn't blend with the over-long sideburns and Mexican-style moustache. The passenger door opened and a woman got out. As she turned Louise realized it was her daughter, Dora, wrapped in a grey fur coat and sporting a short, razor-cut hairdo. The hair looked, Louise noted, like copper wire.

She was at the front door a second after it was knocked. She swung it open and saw Dora switch on a replica of daughterly affection.

'Hello, Mum.' She kissed Louise on the cheek and stepped aside. 'This is Arnold.'

'Pleased to meet you, Mrs Beale.' His handshake was slack and fleeting. Even in this weather it felt warm and moist.

'I thought it was time we popped over and got you two acquainted,' Dora explained.

'Come on in then,' Louise said. 'I'll make a cup of somethin' to warm you.'

'No need to, Mrs Beale.' As they were shown into the

front room Arnold produced a paper-wrapped bottle from his coat pocket. He held it out. 'A little something to cement our meeting.'

'What's this?' Louise took the bottle and turned it in her hands, as if her fingers might be able to read through the wrapping.

'It's Asti, Mum. You'll like it. It's a bit like champagne.'

'Champagne?' Louise uncovered the white foil top. 'It's a bit early in the day for me, love . . .'

'You'll have no trouble with that, Mrs Beale.' Arnold took off his hat, revealing a mass of dark, wavy hair. Louise thought it looked like a cat sitting on his head. 'I chose it specially – light, moderately dry, refreshing.'

'Oh.'

'Arnold's in the wine business, Mum,' Dora said with some pride. 'He manages a shop in West Kensington.'

'Hope to have my own soon,' Arnold added hastily.

Louise stood looking at the bottle, wondering how to cope with it. In her second-hand experience of champagne bottles, the top flew off when they were fiddled with and the stuff poured out all over the place.

'Let Arnold open it,' Dora said, 'an' you can get some glasses, eh?'

'Right.' Louise relinquished the bottle and moved off towards the kitchen. 'I don't think I've got the right kind for champagne, but I'll see what I can dig out.'

As she rummaged in the cupboard beside the sink Louise reminded herself she must be thankful for small mercies. For years, at a distance, she had endured Dora's changes of partner, watching the quality of her taste and attraction gradually fall off. Between the ages of sixteen and eighteen the girl had been out with a bewildering number of men. After she had moved into her own place there was no saying how many there had been. All that was apparent, on the few occasions Louise saw the boyfriends, was that her daughter definitely wasn't attracting the cream. This one was the worst she had seen yet, but at least he was going to marry Dora.

107

Arnold struck Louise as a man taking a lot of trouble to avoid looking like a loser. Maybe he was a man who didn't even know he was a loser. But he was. Just like her brother Terence. He had the same stamp, he was out of the same dead-ender mould.

This one spoke posh but it was put-on posh, which sounded, somehow, a lot further from posh than plain Cockney. His clothes sat on him awkwardly, as if they were ashamed to be on him. His eyes were deep-set and lifeless. And as for the poncy hairstyle . . .

He didn't even begin to fool Louise. Neither did Dora. She could make out she'd been waiting all these years for Mr Right, she could try to give the impression she had saved herself for somebody special. She could even pretend Arnold was a prime catch. It wouldn't impress Louise. She reckoned Dora had landed the best she could, which wasn't much, and she'd done it just in time – even to a mother's compassionate eye, the girl was beginning to look pretty rough.

'I hope these'll do.' Louise came back with three green-stemmed hock glasses and put them on the table. 'I won six of them in a raffle.'

'They'll do just fine,' Arnold said. He had torn away the foil and loosened the wire cage around the cork of the bottle. 'There's a bit of a knack to opening these quietly, without spilling any,' he told Dora, who took in the information with the rapt attentiveness of an acolyte. 'Gentle persuasion, that's the thing, with a deft bit of force as it starts to move.'

Both women watched as, with contorted features, Arnold twisted at the cork. He twisted harder. His face turned pink with the effort, but the cork refused to budge. 'Staff,' he muttered irritably, readjusting his grip. 'I distinctly said I wanted one that had been stored on its side.' He looked at Louise. 'The cork's got dry, you see.'

'Oh. It needs to be wet then, does it?'

'Oh yes. Very important, that.'

As Arnold wrenched again, harshly this time, the cork shot out with a loud pop. Wine frothed over the neck of the bottle and showered on to the table.

'Bugger it!' Arnold yelped. 'Sorry. Language.' He cupped a hand to the neck and tried to pour the froth into the glasses. The wine overflowed from his fingers and more of it dribbled on the table. 'I'm really very sorry, Mrs Beale . . . The sudden change of temperature, I think it's sort of . . .'

'That's all right,' Louise muttered. She went off to fetch a cloth.

After some mopping up and another attempt, Arnold finally managed to pour each of them a glassful. He raised his aloft and frowned at the colour for a moment, then he beamed at the women in turn.

'Here's to us,' he said. 'To your long life and good health, Mrs Beale, and to me and Dora and our long, happy life together as man and wife.'

As they clinked glasses Louise chuckled to cover her self-consciousness. When they had drunk, Arnold asked her what she thought of the wine.

'Nice,' Louise said. She thought it tasted a lot like fruit salts. 'Very nice.'

'There'll be plenty of it at the weddin', Mum,' Dora said.

'Oh, well, that'll be somethin' to look forward to, won't it? Now why don't you sit down an' tell me all about the weddin'? When are you thinkin' of havin' it, anyway?'

'Next month,' Arnold said, smoothing the back of his coat before he sank into an armchair. 'Nothing formal, we decided. Registry office and a party afterwards. I always think big flashy ceremonies are pointless. I mean, as long as you *get* married, what does it matter how you do it?'

Louise thought otherwise but she nodded.

'We're goin' to live in Arnold's flat,' Dora said. 'It's over the shop. Nice an' roomy.'

'It'll do for the time being,' Arnold said airily. 'I've got plans for something much bigger and a lot better. Nothing but the best for your daughter, Mrs Beale.'

Dora tutted softly. 'He spoils me rotten.'

'Well, don't complain about it, girl. Take all the spoilin' you can get, while it's goin'.' Especially from that one, she thought. Wine shops advertised in the papers every week for managers. They seemed to be a footloose breed.

Arnold looked at his glittery wristwatch. 'I hope you don't think I'm bein' rude, Mrs Beale, but I'll have to dash in a minute. I've work to do, you see. Dora thought she'd stop for a while and go over the guest list with you.'

'If that's all right, Mum.'

''Course it is. A nice long chat'll keep me mind off the weather.'

'I think there's just time for us to polish off the rest of the Asti before I go,' Arnold said, reaching for the bottle. Louise watched him pour and wondered if maybe he was a boozer, on top of everything else.

Later, when Arnold had gone and the two women had worked out a rough guest list, Dora raised the subject of money.

'Arnold thought a straight fifty-fifty arrangement would be fairest.'

Louise stared at her. 'Fifty-fifty for what?'

'The reception. I mean, it's tradition that the bride's family pays all the costs, isn't it? Arnold wouldn't hear of that, mind you. He said he'd be glad to foot half the bill an' wouldn't take no for an answer.'

Louise could imagine him saying it, the shifty yob. 'I thought since you'd made all your arrangements already,' she said, 'an' since you don't exactly live here, you an' Arnold would be layin' the whole thing on yourselves.'

'Oh, Mum.' Dora looked hurt. 'Fair's fair. I'm out of a job right now. We can't saddle Arnold with all of it.'

The word 'we' didn't sound right to Louise. For nearly ten years Dora had existed separately, leading a life quite remote from the others'. She had shown no sign of wishing to be an active part of the family. At birthdays and Christmas none of the others expected nor received any cards or gifts from her. She flitted in and out of their lives less frequently than some strangers did.

'How much was you thinkin' about?'

'Well, we worked it out carefully. Seein' as there's goin' to be as many comin' from Arnold's side as ours, a hundred an' twenty quid seems about right.'

'What – for the lot?'

Dora frowned. 'Of course not. Our half, that is. An' that's gettin' it cheap, really. Arnold's got contacts.'

Louise stared at the wall for a moment. 'Well,' she sighed, 'I'll have to talk to your brothers an' see what we can scrape together. I ain't got that kind of money.'

Dora's expression veered towards disbelief. 'I'd have thought you'd a fair bit put away.'

'You know what thought did. I just scrape by most of the time, like a lot of folk round here.' Louise looked across and caught a glimpse of the old Dora, the fretful, suspicious child who took nothing at face value, who accepted no argument until she had tested it to full stretch.

She sniffed. 'I suppose the rest of the family have all had their share out of you already.'

'Meanin', I suppose, that you haven't.'

'Well . . .'

'Listen,' Louise said, 'the rest of them, they've kept puttin' a lot into this household over the years. They don't forget their mum. Just because there's only Pauline livin' here now, it don't mean she's the only one helpin' out with the upkeep.'

'I've had to look after *meself*, Mum,' Dora complained. 'I haven't had me brothers an' sister rallyin' round all the time . . .'

'Well it looks like they'll have to now, don't it?' Louise slapped her hand firmly on the arm of her chair. 'Look, I

111

don't want to start squabblin' over this. You're gettin' married, that's what we're talkin' about, not who's got what or why. So. Leave it with me. I'll talk to the boys. Enough said.'

Dora did her best to look contrite. 'I'm sorry, Mum. I've just been a bit nervous over the whole thing. It's a big step I'm takin', after all.'

They fell silent for a minute. Dora gazed at the guest list on her knees, Louise stared out at the snow. Then Dora cleared her throat.

'Mum, about the money. I'd like to have it off you in a couple of weeks, if that's all right.'

'How come?'

'Well, Arnold says if he can have it then, he'll pay cash in advance for everythin' an' get the extra discount.'

Louise watched the swirling snowflakes again. She wondered how desperate it might get. Would there be times when Dora would come running to her, penniless, begging the price of Arnold's booze bills, or his gambling debts, or his petty-theft fines? Would there be sums begged so that big opportunities could be taken, with promises of swift repayment that would never materialize?

'I'll do what I can,' Louise said flatly.

Maybe the couple would fare better than that, she mused. They might manage to stagger from one emergency to another and keep getting by, if only by the skin of their teeth.

She diverted her mind from the depressing possibilities and sat back in her chair, her eyes fixed on the empty wine bottle.

After a minute Dora said, 'What're you dreamin' about, Mum?' Her voice had taken on the friendly, best-chum tone she always used when she had managed to wangle her own way over something.

'Nothin',' Louise said. 'Nothin' at all.' In truth, a

112

thought had occurred to her suddenly and she was considering it when Dora interrupted. She wondered if the undulant wodge of hair on Arnold's head was in fact a wig. If it was, how much more terrible did he look without it?

At four o'clock that afternoon Pete Beale came out through the gates of the yard where he worked and found Pat standing there. She had brought a pushchair with the younger boy, Simon, wrapped up inside. Only his forehead showed above the edge of the waterproof cover. David stood alongside, sullen and glowering, holding his mother's hand.

'What're you doin' here?' Pete asked her.

'It's pay day, isn't it?' Pat wore no make-up. The cold had turned her face a dusty blue-beige colour.

'What's wrong with gettin' your money the usual way?' Normally he put the cash in an envelope and left it at the sub post office, in the care of a woman who was related to Pat. 'You're not plannin' on showin' up here every Friday, are you?'

Already, to Pete's embarrassment, a number of people he worked with had come by, looking sidelong at Pat and the kids and nudging one another.

'If I want to come an' get my money direct, I'm entitled to.'

'Now don't start that, Pat . . .'

'I'll bring a copper with me, if I have to.'

'Don't be so piggin' stupid,' he hissed, winning a dark scowl from David.

'I'm just tellin' you, in case you think you can stay away from us an' not have to see me an' the kids at all.' She held out her hand. 'Let's have it, then.'

Pete looked about him cautiously. 'Come round the corner.'

'I'll have it here. An' I'm in a hurry. I don't want my kids catchin' pneumonia out in all this snow.'

'Then you shouldn't have brought them out, should you?' Pete fished the wage packet from his pocket and tore off the end. He turned aside as he counted off the right amount, then handed it to Pat.

'Looks like you've kept plenty for yourself.' She snatched the money and put it in her purse.

'Listen, Pat . . .' He paused until some people went past. 'You're *not* goin' to be standin' here every Friday, are you? It makes me look a right tit in front of me mates . . .'

'I shouldn't think you'd look much different if I wasn't here.'

She hadn't lost any of her old style, Pete reflected. How could he ever have thought he loved her? How had he walked into the jaws of misery with both eyes open?

'As it happens,' Pat said, 'I came here today because I've somethin' to tell you.'

'What?' She's got cancer, he thought fancifully. She's got a blood disease and she's got hardly any time to live. She's found another bloke . . .

'I've found out about you an' that Kathy Hills.'

He stared at her, trying to keep his face expressionless. 'You what?'

'I've got proof. An' my lawyer's gettin' to hear about it. That'll put a different look on your divorce papers.'

'I don't know what you're on about,' he said. To his own ears his voice sounded hollow. 'Straight I don't.'

'Is that a fact?' Pat jerked the pushchair round and aimed it in the direction of the shops. 'You know all right. An' before long everybody'll know. Your old mum, for starters. I'll see to that.'

'Now Pat – '

She marched off, her boots crunching on the snow, young David throwing a parting glare. Pete stood watching them, his ears pounding, stomach swirling.

Would it ever end, he wondered? Even now when he was away from her, out of her presence – right out of her life, in fact – he was still in a position to be hurt, to be *mangled* by that woman. He felt the old nightmare days closing in on him again, those dark, hesitant stretches of time when all he sensed ahead of him was another bombshell, primed to go off in his face.

12

At first, the thought of missing the wedding had upset Pauline. It wasn't just that she had bought new clothes and wouldn't be able to show them off. She had prepared herself mentally for the celebration, seeing it as a highly welcome bright spot in a gloomy, dreary winter.

The 'flu had hit her two days before the big event. She tried to hide it at first, but her mother had caught on fast. She took one look at the dark-rimmed eyes, the feverish tremor, the unhealthy flush.

'Bed, my girl. You're in no fit state to go anywhere.'

As the infection developed, Pauline became quite glad she had obeyed Louise's order – not that she'd had any option. The way she felt, she would probably have passed out before Dora and Arnold had said 'I do'. She would have spoiled the whole day for everybody.

Now, on the day of the wedding, Pauline felt no regrets at all. The whole thing was obviously going to be a disaster and well worth missing. The day before, Dora had turned up and asked for more money. From her bed upstairs Pauline had eavesdropped on the row that followed. Louise let it all out – what she thought of Arnold, of Dora and of their doom-laden prospects as a married couple.

In the end money did change hands, however. Louise, as usual, had an emergency sum tucked away and she gave it to Dora, saying that she was only doing it because she didn't want the disgrace of a tuppenny-ha'penny reception on her elder daughter's wedding day.

After that things got worse. Kenny, who had agreed to be one of the witnesses, had gone round to the hall where the reception was to be held. His nose took him there, he told his mother afterwards. It had all smelt dodgy to him. What he found confirmed his suspicions. All Dora's talk about lashings of food and drink had been nonsense, no more than a pack of lies. The caretaker, readily accepting Kenny's credentials, showed him what had been laid on. There were two cases of Spanish wine, a half bottle each of whisky, gin and vodka and four crates of bottled beer.

'That ain't the worst of it, though,' Kenny said. 'That brammer Arnold's got the caretaker an' his wife to lay on the food. He's told them he'll shell out ten quid, tops.'

'But where's all the money gone?' Louise demanded.

'Oh, that's not much of a mystery. Arnold's been swankin' a bit about the honeymoon. Showed the caretaker the plane tickets an' hotel reservations. Majorca, two weeks.'

Lying in bed now, comforting herself with a cup of hot lemon, Pauline foresaw a terrible showdown. Her mother had been grimly quiet for the entire morning. She was getting her wrath on the boil.

The door opened and Louise poked her head into the room. She was ready to go, her flowery, veiled hat perched squarely on her head.

'Are you decent?'

Pauline glanced down at her high-necked flannelette nightdress. 'Nobody could be more decent than this, Mum.'

'Right. I've got a visitor to see you.' She pushed the door wider and ushered Arthur Fowler inside.

'Thought I'd try an' cheer you up,' he mumbled, clearly uneasy in the intimate surroundings of his girlfriend's bedroom.

'Just don't get up to anythin',' Louise said grumpily, making Arthur blush. 'I'm goin' now.'

'Enjoy yourself, Mum.'

'Like hell I will.' Louise banged the door shut.

Arthur moved to the side of the bed. 'How do you feel?'

'Horrible. I've got a head full of porridge an' when I cough me lungs sound like an explosion in an accordion factory.'

Arthur was looking around for a chair. The only one in the room was piled high with clothes.

'Sit on the bed. I'm sure Mum won't come runnin' back in to check up on us.'

He lowered himself gently on the edge and reached for Pauline's hand. It was his favourite gesture of affection, just holding her hand in his; it was the only one he ever displayed in public.

'I get the impression the weddin's goin' to be a let-down for everybody,' he said. 'Your Mum's rumblin' a bit dangerously.'

'She'll wait till they're hitched before she lets them have it. They'll get both barrels, I shouldn't doubt. They deserve it.' She handed Arthur her empty cup and he put it on the bedside table. 'There's been a heck of a lot of heartache through weddin's in this family.'

'What can you expect?' Arthur said. 'Pete, he got married for all the wrong reasons, an' far too young at that. Your Dora – well, she's just grabbin' who she can get. An' her bloke's doin' the same, if what your Mum says is anythin' to go by.'

Pauline nodded, dabbing the pink tip of her nose with a tissue. 'People go out of their way to be miserable, a lot of the time.'

Arthur's fingers tightened around hers. 'Are you miserable, love?'

'In this state I am.'

'No, I mean, when you're not laid up. Are you happy in yourself? Happy with the way things are, or do you fancy a bit more out of life?'

It was unusual for Arthur to talk this way. His style, usually, was to restrict his conversation to the superficial aspects of life. Pauline had never known him to broach the topic of his emotions, or hers. Nowadays they kissed

118

and cuddled a fair amount, but they never talked about the reasons behind those gentle urges.

'I suppose I get fed up, sometimes. It's only natural. My job's boring . . .'

She lopped off the rest of the sentence – *my free time's boring, too.* She never actively thought of it any more, she simply accepted that her life was pretty flat, compared to other girls'.

'There's some things I'd like to change, I suppose,' she said. 'But not many.'

'How about me?' Arthur murmured.

'You?'

'Would you want to change me?' He was blushing again, avoiding her eyes.

'Change you? Make you different, you mean?'

'I mean change me for somebody else.'

Pauline inhaled sharply, preparing to reply, but she inhaled too deeply and brought on a coughing fit. Arthur slapped her back gently until the spasm subsided.

'Oh Lord,' she groaned, wiping her streaming eyes. 'What a mess I'm in, eh?' She looked at Arthur's solemn face and smiled at him. 'Of course I don't want to change you. That was a daft thing to say, wasn't it?'

'Just wondered.'

'I should think you'd want to swop me, the state I'm in.'

He squeezed her hand again. 'I'd never want to change you. Never.'

She was touched. It was the sweetest thing Arthur had ever said to her.

'Pauline.' He paused, frowning at the quilt as if he'd discovered a moth hole. 'Pauline . . .' He looked up. 'Do you fancy gettin' married?'

Beneath her sudden confusion, she was aware that this really fitted her picture. It happened differently to other girls; they were taken out, they were surrounded with music and glamorous lights and *then* their men proposed

119

to them. But here she was, bunged with 'flu, looking like a hurricane had hit her, propped up in bed in her dowdiest nightie . . .

'Well . . .'

She hadn't dwelt much on the thought of marriage. A long time ago, though, she had realized that all she really wanted was a husband and a family – and to be allowed to stay in the place where she grew up.

'I'm not tryin' to rush you for an answer, love.'

She smiled. Where was the sense in delay, when she knew already what she wanted? 'Yes, Arthur. I'd like to get married.'

He beamed at her. 'Great.' He leaned forward and kissed her. 'Don't care if I catch 'flu,' he said, squeezing both of her hands now. 'You won't change your mind, will you?'

'Not likely.'

'When'll we do it?'

'It?' she squeaked, putting on a false look of alarm.

'You know what I mean.'

Pauline thought for a minute, trying to be practical through the invading haze of pleasure. 'I think we best leave it till late in the year. Let Mum get used to the idea.'

Louise didn't dislike Arthur, though she did think he was a bit wet, and she was suspicious about his background. 'He comes from a rough old turnin',' she had warned Pauline years ago. 'It's a well-known district for villains an' punch-ups.' In time, though, Louise had learned that Arthur was honest, straightforward and loyal. It would probably be some compensation, Pauline thought, for her mother to know that she, like Ronnie, wanted to marry and settle down with somebody reliable.

'We'll have lots to plan, now,' Arthur grinned.

'I'll say.' Pauline was really feeling the new condition settle on her now. She was an engaged person. She had never thought she would feel as different as this.

'Arthur – how long have you been plannin' on askin' me?'

'I didn't plan it.' His smile was almost apologetic. 'I surprised meself.'

'Really? You hadn't been gatherin' the courage or nothin' like that?'

'I came round to cheer you up. That was all. It just sort of came over me.'

'Like the 'flu?'

'A bit like that, yeah.'

'Oh, Arthur.' Pauline pushed herself forward, put out her arms and wrapped them around him.

Arnold had caught the atmosphere of hostility immediately after the ceremony. Accordingly, he kept himself surrounded by friends as he circulated at the reception, moving about the grimy little hall like a mafioso walled-in by henchmen. Dora, too, kept close to an unsavoury-looking group of men and women and made only glancing contact with members of her own family.

'A right bloody rip-off,' was Kenny's verdict when it was all over. He stood in the emptying hall with his mother and Pete, watching the caretaker stacking chairs at the back of the platform. 'All them two was after was some money. If they hadn't been, they'd have got married on the quiet. They wouldn't have bothered to invite us.'

'I'll have that little bitch yet,' Louise swore.

It had been her plan to take Dora aside at the first opportunity, Arnold too, and give them a thorough scalding. But the couple had slipped out to their car without telling anybody, leaving it to one of Arnold's bulky, mouth-breathing friends to announce that the couple were now leaving, if anybody wanted to see them off. The car was turning the corner by the time Louise got outside.

'Two sandwiches I've had,' Pete grunted. 'Two. I never even smelt the beer.'

'It was a disgrace,' Louise snapped. 'An' who the hell were all them hangers-on? As far as I could see, Arnold didn't have any relatives here at all.'

'They're the jet set him an' Dora hang out with, Mum,' Kenny said. 'Bunch of bloody reject strip-club barkers, by the look of them. God knows what Dora's lettin' herself in for.'

'She knows well enough,' Louise assured him. 'If you ask me, they deserve one another.'

Kenny wandered across the room to have a word with Ronnie and Gail. Louise turned to Pete. 'Well? Are you behavin' yourself, like you was told?'

'Yes, Mum,' he groaned. 'I wasn't misbehavin', anyway. I'm entitled to have an innocent drink or two with a girl if I want to.'

'You're still a married man,' she reminded him. 'As for havin' an innocent drink – well, that's not the way it was told to me.'

It had been told to her, in fact, in an ill-written, one-page anonymous letter which quite obviously came from Pat. The note declared that Pete was 'carrying on with that slut Kathy Hills' and that his wife's solicitor was going to take the appropriate action – or, as the note said, 'do him for it'.

'It's bad enough you've got the name you have round the district, without buildin' yourself a reputation for hangin' around with loose women.'

'Kathy Hills isn't a loose woman, Mum. The only loose one I ever knew was Pat.'

'Then you shouldn't have married her.'

'I didn't know until after we were married.'

Louise pursed her lips, considering whether to give voice to a question that had troubled her for a long time. She decided she would. 'Tell me somethin'. She wasn't really pregnant when you got married, was she?'

'No.'

'So she said she was in the club just to hook you?'

'That's right. But it was a bit worse than that. She married me to spite another bloke.'

Louise looked outraged. 'What other bloke?'

'Some married man she'd been knockin' about with. He'd promised her he'd divorce his wife, but he couldn't go through with it. Pat told me all about it one night, just to lay on an extra bit of torture.'

'My God, the things you hear.' Louise shook her head. 'When all's said an' done, though, slag as she might be, Pat's your wife. An' them two kids are yours, too. I don't hold with this divorce lark, Pete. It's never happened in this family before.'

'There's got to be a first time for everythin'.'

'No there hasn't!'

Pete shrugged. 'I'm goin' through with it, anyway.'

Louise sighed. 'I've had enough for one day. I'm goin' home. I'm gettin' out of these clothes an' into somethin' comfortable, then I'm goin' to have a drink in the Vic with Ethel.' She waved her arm at the hall. 'I've got to get the taste of this shambles out of me mouth.'

They parted at the door. Without comment, Pete took in his mother's warning, again, to behave himself, kissed her on the cheek and said he'd pop round to see her over the weekend.

Ten minutes later, he let himself into his little flat. He hung up his jacket and eased the knot in his tie. Kicking off his shoes, he padded along the short hallway and into the living room.

'Afternoon, madam,' he said brightly. 'I'm from the sanitary. I've come about the smell on the landin'.'

Kathy had been drowsing. She stretched and stood up, letting her magazine slide to the floor. They embraced tightly.

'How did it go?' she asked as Pete nuzzled her hair.

'Terrible. A total fiasco from start to finish. How long have you been here?'

'Half an hour.'

'Your folks say anythin'?'

'Not today.' Kathy eased away from him, smoothing her flared skirt. 'But there'll be more said yet. There's bound to be.'

'I'm sorry about it, love. All of it. Really I am.'

'You've nothing to be sorry for, Pete. I knew what I was lettin' meself in for. I'm not some little innocent you led astray.'

'You're not what they're sayin' you are, either.'

The gossip around the district had been imaginative and vicious. Kathy and Pete had been seen together in public no more than three times. On those occasions there had been no outward displays of anything between them but friendliness.

That had been enough, however, to spark bonfires of speculation and innuendo. Pete was pointed out as a thorough-going bastard, a married man who had left his wife and children and was now in the erotic clutches of the newly labelled Whore of Walford. Kathy's father had actually hit her when he heard the rumours. One of her brothers vowed he'd batter Pete first chance he got. Neighbours watched Kathy warily and dropped sarcastic, wounding remarks as she passed them on the street.

'I don't really give a toss what anybody says, or thinks,' she said.

'Yes you do,' Pete murmured.

She stepped close to him again and put her arms around his neck. 'OK, I do, now and then. I cry me eyes out some nights.'

'How long do you think you can stick it?'

'As long as I have to.' She pecked his nose. 'Anyway, a lot of what they say is dead right. I *am* a brazen cow. That night in the pub I threw myself at you. I went there deliberately to do it.'

Pete's face was very serious. 'You reckon you can put up with it all, then? I mean, it could get worse.'

124

'Don't worry about me.' She kissed him again. 'I'm one bird you're stuck with, no matter what happens.'

Pete buried his face in her hair. He prayed, earnestly, that she was right.

13

In October Pauline and Arthur were married. Throughout the previous months they'd had no luck with their house-hunting. The trouble was that they could only afford to rent, and the rent they could afford was not high. Their expectations began to dim as they viewed one miserable, rundown dwelling after another.

A month before the wedding Louise made a suggestion. It was geared to help the couple and to solve her own worries about being left alone in the house. They could move in with her, she told them.

Arthur was reluctant. Pauline had misgivings, too. They talked it over and finally came to the conclusion that Louise's offer was their best prospect. The alternative was to rent rooms in some damp, dingy, rat-ridden old house in the poor end of the borough.

Four days after they were married, following a brief honeymoon in Eastbourne, Pauline and Arthur moved in with Louise.

'It's not so bad,' Arthur told one of his mates at the factory. By then, he had been living at number forty-five for a month. 'Just as long as I don't get in the old girl's way, she's no trouble. An' it's quite nice, livin' in a house with all the comforts ready laid on.'

The arrangement worked well from Louise's point of view, too. She still had Pauline around the house to talk to in the evenings. Arthur was the kind of man who didn't make heavy demands on his wife's time, so there was no ill-feeling if the two women chattered an entire evening away and left him to sit by the fire with his newspaper.

'He's a bit set in his ways for a young man, mind you,'

Louise confided to Ethel Skinner. 'He's only twenty-six, but you'd think he was twice as old sometimes. He comes in, washes, gets changed, eats his food an' then drops into the chair with his paper or a library book. I'm not complainin', mind you. It's just that I'd thought our Pauline would marry a man with more go about him.'

Pauline, for her part, had never been more content. Contentment, in fact, was what she had wanted most. Marriage to Arthur gave her the cosy sense of being settled into a lasting, satisfactory way of life. Sharing her mother's house was nowhere near as difficult as she had feared, and there were a lot of advantages to the arrangement. One day, she supposed, they would have a house of their own, but for the time being she felt no urgent need to make plans in that direction.

At the laundry, Pauline assured the other girls that her Arthur was turning out to be everything a husband should be. He had all the virtues, she told them – all the ones that mattered, anyway. There were even things about him that reminded her of her father; he was considerate, gentle, naturally wise. Perhaps he could be a shade too predictable at times, and he needed coaxing to take her out at weekends, but she couldn't have everything, she reasoned.

Two days before Christmas Dr Legg told Pauline that she was pregnant. Louise began knitting the same day. When Arthur came home and was given the news, he told Pauline he couldn't have had a nicer Christmas present. Louise told him, with darkly hinting eyes, that he'd better be gentle with the girl from now on.

For a lot of people in the borough who could afford it, the week from Christmas to the end of the year was a time of steady celebration, rather than a gap between festivities. The bars and clubs rang nightly with the shouting, laughter and singing of people determined to make up for the drudgery, strain and toil that had brought them to this time of release.

To the older people in Walford, as in every other part of Britain, the celebrations of Christmas and New Year's Eve were like safe harbours. At those times they could pause to look forward and back. They could remind themselves of who they were and how they stood in relation to each other.

For Den Watts, too, that New Year's Eve was a time of self-assessment. It reminded him of who he was – Den the Lad, slick-tongued, sharp-witted, a smooth-dressing self-styled ladies' man, who was also as near a virgin as made no difference and was secretly very shy with people. This time also made him painfully aware of how he stood in relation to Angie Watts; one hour from midnight, he was being invited to put his talent where his mouth was.

A year after the night she had invited him to kiss her – and, a little later, had invited him to do more, which yet again he couldn't manage – Den was being given another chance. His *third* that year, he reminded himself. The responsibility was overwhelming. He was desperate to succeed with Angie, but at the same time he wanted, just as desperately, to run away and hide.

It was their first date in eight months. They were on the back seat of a Ford Consul Den had borrowed for the evening. They had moved into the back at Angie's suggestion, because it would be more comfortable there, she said coyly. She lay relaxed and kittenishly supple along cushions, while Den half-sat, half-lay beside her. He felt so taut he was sure one wrong move would crack a bone.

'What have you been doin' with yourself all this time, anyway?' Angie asked, breaking the awkward, brittle silence.

'A bit of wheelin', bit of dealin',' he said. It was a convenient summary. To tell her all he had been doing would take a long time and he wouldn't come out of the story looking very good – not without performing a lot of surgery on the truth, anyway. 'How about you?'

128

'Driftin',' Angie sighed. 'I've had a couple of jobs, a boyfriend or two.'

And she had probably just broken up with one of them, Den thought. That was what had happened when she played up to him a year ago, and again in April. This time, she had approached him in a café and had more or less engineered their date.

'I know people shouldn't drift,' she said, 'but I've not got the plans for my life worked out yet,' She paused, frowning in the shadows. 'It's like buildin' a house, isn't it? You've got to gather the bits together before you can get weavin'.'

Distracted and uncomfortable as he was, Den wanted to argue with that. 'I look at it different. I reckon you should decide the kind of house you want to put up, then start buildin' it right away. You can collect the bits as you go.'

'So you've got your plans made, have you?'

'Yeah.'

'What kind of house is it?'

'A skyscraper.'

Angie raised one knee. The hem of her skirt slid along her thigh. Den gulped softly.

'I like a man that knows where he's goin'.' She stroked his cheek with the tips of her fingers.

'A bloke's got to have ambitions,' Den murmured. His throat felt terribly dry. 'An' he should always plan big.'

'I suppose, when I think about it,' Angie said huskily, 'I'd sooner be part of somebody else's plans than make too many of me own.'

'That ain't a bad thing.'

'Talkin' of plans . . .' She moved again, settling deeper into the upholstery, making the springs creak. 'Have you any in mind for the next ten minutes or so?' Her hands went to his shoulders, drawing him down.

Panic bells went off all over Den's head. This was a

mismatch. He was 18 and she was 21. To Den, that three-year gap seemed more like thirty, in terms of experience. Angie's experience terrified him.

'Come on,' she urged him. She took his hand and guided it to her leg. It lay there like a sculpture. 'Come *on*.'

Blindly he began to put together the motions, tried to make them blend. He conjured every aid in his imagination to get him over the hurdle between ambition and performance. For five ghastly, nightmarish minutes Den struggled to do what everybody was supposed to do by simple instinct. Finally, crushingly, he admitted defeat and moved away from the panting Angie.

There was a long, terrible silence.

Finally Angie spoke. 'I don't believe any of this.' She sat up and rearranged her clothing. 'You should see a bloody doctor.'

'I'm sorry . . .' Words failed him. They had the last time, too. And the time before.

'Is it me, or what?'

'No, it's not you.'

Angie sighed. At least, he observed, she wasn't as mad this time. 'Does it happen when you're with other girls?'

'No. Yes. I mean – '

'It's downright unnatural.'

He sighed.

'Den. Listen to me. Have you ever wondered why I go out with you?'

He said nothing.

'I take one look at you an' I think, that guy looks really smart. He's got a lot of chat an' charm. He's got style. Him an' me would make a great-lookin' couple. So I try to make it happen. I keep on tryin' even though I tell myself I should forget it.' She peered at him. 'If you don't want us to team up, Den, why don't you just tell me? Why do we have to go through all this?'

Confession, the soul-baring, utterly truthful kind, was

something Den avoided. He was horrified by the very thought of anybody knowing anything about the person he really was. Yet now he knew he was going to spill the truth to Angie. He couldn't help himself. He had hit the bottom and he could only ever get up again if he unloaded his burden of make-believe.

'I've not done it before,' he blurted.

'What? Never?'

'Not properly. I get nervous with you. I'm scared I'll do it wrong.' He tensed himself, waiting for the ridicule.

'I don't believe that.'

'It's true.'

Angie considered the information. 'I knew you were all mouth when you were younger,' she said finally, 'but I thought you'd picked up a bit of experience since then. I'd have sworn it. I mean, the way you come on heavy – '

'That's just the mouth again,' he said. 'An' I can put on the flash when I want. It's all top show. There's nothin' under it.'

Again Den waited, wondering if she would taunt him, or maybe just get out of the car and walk home. He was deeply surprised when she leaned close to him and kissed his cheek.

'Nobody else knows, do they?' she whispered.

'Not a soul.'

'That's all right then.' She sat back and pulled him with her. 'Now, before we go any further, let's get this straight. You *do* fancy me, don't you?'

'A bit more than plenty.'

'Fine. Because I keep fancyin' you, in spite of everythin'. What I said is straight, you know – I think we'd make a great-lookin' pair.'

Confessing, Den began to think, had probably been a good move.

'This little problem you've got is all that's gettin' in the way,' she went on. 'An' it's no problem at all, now I

know what it is.' She laughed softly. 'I was really startin'
to take it personal.'

'You . . . You reckon it'll get sorted out?' he said
awkwardly.

'Definitely.' She turned and put her arms around him.
'It'll be sorted out before you're back in that drivin' seat.'

In the darkness Den smiled, feeling as confident, suddenly, as Angie did.

Kathy Hills turned to Pete at the corner of the dark
street and kissed him swiftly. 'Right,' she said. 'I'll go the
rest of the way on me own.'

'Are you sure?'

'I'm sure. I told you not to come out, anyway.'

'I didn't like the idea of you walkin' the streets on your
own tonight. There's a lot of drunks about.'

'Off you go an' get drunk yourself.' She kissed him
again. 'I'll see you tomorrow.'

He watched her disappear into the darkness, then
turned and moved off in the direction he had come.

· For Pete the anniversary was tinged with disappointment. A year ago he had brought in the new year with
Kathy. Tonight, he had taken her part of the way to her
house a full half hour before midnight.

There had been no sensible alternative. As long as
they kept their relationship low-key, there would be no
trouble. Kathy's family now believed she had stopped
seeing Pete. His family, he was sure, believed the same.
He would have preferred the affair to be conducted less
furtively, but for the moment furtive was the way it had
to stay.

He walked briskly through the dark streets, heading
for the traditional party at the Queen Victoria. He had
never felt less like going to a party, but appearances had
to be maintained. If he didn't show up at the pub,
his mother's bloodhound instincts would start operating
again.

132

'Hoi! You! Beale!'

He stopped and looked across the road. The call had come from a doorway, recessed beyond the reach of the street light.

'Who's that?'

A man stepped out on to the pavement. Another one followed him. They came across the road slowly. At three yards Pete recognized the taller man. It was Colin Hills, one of Kathy's brothers. He stopped directly in front of Pete. His companion stood beside him.

'You think you're a fly man, don't you?' Colin said.

'What are you talkin' about?'

'We saw you, bugger-lugs. Five minutes ago. You was with our Kath.'

Pete shook his head. 'Not me, mate.'

'Yes *you*, mate. We both saw you. We've been waitin' for you to come back.' He moved closer. 'You know it's against the rules, don't you? She's been told not to see you, an' you've been warned to keep your distance from her.'

Pete recalled the warning. It had been issued loudly from a car that passed him one morning on his way to work.

Colin turned his large head slowly and looked at the other man. 'What do you do about that, George? What's to be done when a bloke don't take a tellin'?'

'Tell him harder,' George rumbled.

'That's what I reckoned.'

Pete got ready to run. George's hand shot out and grabbed his arm.

'Get your bleedin' mitt off me!'

'You should've listened first time,' Colin grunted beerily.

'Listen, I was only – '

Colin's knee thudded into Pete's groin.

'Aah! Jesus!'

Pain flared and tugged Pete to his knees. As he sank

133

George punched the side of his head, knocking his face into the path of Colin's hurtling fist. Pete heard a crack and saw the street lamps jolt sideways. As his cheek collided with the pavement a boot struck his spine and another one rammed his stomach. In a dizzying swirl of pain and nausea he felt one more kick on his shoulder, then heard the two men hurrying away.

He lay where he was for a long time, trying to vomit, convinced his back had been broken. When he finally managed to sit up the pain in his head swelled and made him cry out. He pushed himself to his feet and began walking, steadying himself with a hand on the wall.

'Bastards,' he grunted. 'Stinkin' bastards.' They could do what they liked, he thought fiercely. They'd have to kill him before he'd stop seeing her. They'd have to dismantle him.

At the corner he stopped, catching his breath, counting the pains as they scissored and sliced through him. He wondered about Kathy. He hoped they wouldn't harm her. If they did, he'd get every last one of them. The whole family if he had to . . .

Across the road an elderly drunk tottered into view. He stopped, stared for a moment at Pete's hunched figure, then waved a hand with a bottle clutched in it.

'Happy New Year, son!' he yelled.

Pete groaned as he heard the bells begin to ring.

14

Harold Legg leaned down over Reg Cox's gaping mouth and shone his torch inside. The tonsils glowed puffily warm behind the furred expanse of tongue.

'All right Reg, you can close it again.' Harold switched off the torch and went back behind his desk. 'I'll give you a prescription for some tablets and a mouthwash.'

'Thanks, Doctor.'

'They'll clear up the infection,' Harold said, beginning to write, 'but they won't solve the problem.' He signed the prescription and passed it across the desk. 'That's the third time it's flared up in a year. You know what's causing the trouble, I told you before.'

Reg nodded glumly, knuckling one watery eye. 'Me teeth.'

'Yes, your teeth. They're badly decayed. Terribly decayed, in fact. If there was a white one in there you'd have a snooker set.' He shook his head. 'They've got to come out some time.'

'I don't hold with dentists.'

'And I'm quite sure dentists don't hold with people like you. Whoever takes that lot out is going to have quite a job on his hands. But if they're left where they are they'll go on being a source of infection. You'll have one bad throat after another. It won't stop at throat trouble, either.'

Reg's face crumpled into a frown. 'I was always taught you should hang on to your teeth, no matter what.'

'When they're in good condition, yes. Or even when they can be restored. Not when they're in that mess. Your teeth have turned against you, Reg. They're poisoning you.'

135

Reg folded the prescription and stood up. 'I'll have a think about it.'

'Don't leave it too long, then.'

Reg hobbled out. Harold put away the case card and rang the bell. A moment later Ronnie Beale came in. He was in his market clothes, wrapped up to the neck against the April winds. He greeted the doctor with his usual shy smile. His eyes, though, were rather guarded.

'Good morning, Ronnie. Come and sit down.' Harold took a folder from the desk and spread it open in front of him as Ronnie took a seat. 'I told you last time, I wanted to think over your case before I decided on a course of treatment.' He tapped a sheet of paper in the folder. 'I also took a bit of advice from a higher quarter.'

'Will I live, then?' Ronnie grinned, but his eyes remained serious.

'You've a better chance than most people.' Harold stared at the paper for a moment. 'A man can go through life with a time bomb in his chest, not knowing that each tick takes it nearer to blowing up. That won't happen to you, because you're monitored regularly. Besides, your heart isn't diseased.'

'I know I asked once before,' Ronnie said slowly, 'but this thing I've got, mitra-whatsit – '

'Mitral stenosis.'

'Does it mean I won't live as long as I would without it?'

'If you don't mind changing your style of living and taking a couple of tablets a day, every day, you'll have a perfectly normal life expectancy. Have you been worrying about that?'

'A bit. Well, a lot. Ever since you told me it'd get worse.'

Harold folded his hands and gave Ronnie his most reassuring smile. 'Your heart isn't growing weaker. It's matured, that's all. Toughened. The narrowed valve is more *stubbornly* narrow now, so we have to take action to make sure it isn't asked to cope with more than it can handle.'

'Will it get narrower yet?'

'In your case, I don't believe so. But if it ever did, there's a straightforward operation that can put matters right. You mustn't worry about it. If you follow the rules, you won't even have any symptoms. Ever.'

Harold had discovered the defective valve over two years before in the course of a routine medical examination. The defect had probably been there since Ronnie's childhood, Harold believed, when it would have been undetectable. Over the past year, during regular check-ups, he had observed that the valve was altering its behaviour. Now it had settled down. He had predicted it would and he had advised Ronnie, well in advance, about the precautions he would need to take.

'How are the plans going for the new life, anyway?'

'Everything's in hand,' Ronnie said.

'Your mother might be a bit difficult about things, of course.'

Ronnie grinned. 'I didn't want to say anythin' to her until we were sure it would all go through. I'll break it very gently.'

'I should, if I were you.' Harold examined the papers in the file for another few seconds, then closed it. 'Right. We'll start you on the tablets straight away. That'll take care of the first half of your treatment. The sooner you take care of the other half, the better.'

'Just a matter of weeks now, Doctor.'

When he had been given his prescription Ronnie went back to the stall on Bridge Street. He felt relieved and reassured by what the doctor had told him and he began eagerly attacking the morning's work.

It was a Friday so he was busy. For two and a half hours he served a steady stream of shoppers, nearly all of them regulars with their own fads and foibles which Ronnie always took pains to accommodate. It was a thriving business and it was perfectly situated. Beale's Fruit 'n' Veg was the last stall on the market and people always bought their vegetables last, because they were the heaviest purchases on a food-shopping trip. The fact that the stall was right beside the Queen Victoria was another advantage; there was nothing nicer than a quick drink when the shopping had all been done.

A few minutes after one o'clock, Ronnie turned from giving a customer change and saw Pete coming along the street from the direction of the bridge. Ronnie had been expecting him. He signalled to young Jackie on the jewellery stall and held up the spread fingers of both hands. Jackie nodded. Ronnie stepped across to the door of the pub and waited for Pete.

'Right,' he said as his brother drew level. 'I've got a ten-minute break. You could use a drink, I suppose.'

'You're a mind reader.'

They stepped inside and were impelled towards the bar by Alf Barrett's broad smile.

'Afternoon, lads. Pints, is it?'

'A pint for Ronnie,' Pete said. 'I'll have a brandy. Large.'

Alf nodded and set about filling the order. Ronnie looked at Pete. 'Brandy. It was that bad, then?'

'I've got very mixed feelings, Ron. One part of me wants to cheer, the other part wants to break it's heart sobbin'.'

They took their drinks to a table and sat down. 'Now then,' Ronnie said when he had taken a gulp from his glass. 'Tell me all.'

Pete moistened his tongue with brandy. 'First of all, when I got to the court I had to sit in an ante-room with a lot of glarin' women. I was the only bloke in the place, an' you could tell what they thought about blokes. Christ. I was glad there was a copper at the door.'

'Did it take long?'

'Once I was in, no, it didn't. The judge got a potted

version of the evidence off the two briefs – you should have heard some of the shit Pat's bloke was flingin' – then he had a bit of a mumbled chat with them, then he said he would grant the divorce. Decree nisi. Decree absolute in three months.'

'You're gettin' good at that legal patter,' Ronnie observed.

'It don't take long to pick up. Anyway, after that he waffled a bit about custody of the kids an' visitin' rights, then he hit me with the maintenance arrangements.'

'Tough, are they?'

'Brutal. I saw Pat, the cow, all smug an' smirkin' on the other side of the room. What with the regular weekly payments, plus quarterly clothing payments an' other odds an' ends, I reckon it'll cost me half me wage.' He swallowed some brandy. 'Still. I'm a free man, Ronnie.'

'Only when the divorce is made absolute,' Ronnie reminded him.

'Yeah, I know. I've got to be careful not to get into bed with Pat durin' that time, or they cancel the lot.' He laughed. 'There's more chance of me havin' it off with Ursula Andress.'

Ronnie took some more of his beer, then he pushed the glass aside and leaned his elbows on the table. 'Well, I'm glad you've got it over with, Pete. It makes things tidy an' final. Now I've some news for you. I didn't get you to come over here just to tell me what happened.'

'It's good news, I hope.'

'It's about that bonus you were promised.'

'For bein' a good lad?' Pete smiled. 'To tell you the truth, I got the feelin' I hadn't qualified for it.'

'You have now.'

'Even with me blottin' the record with Kathy?'

Ronnie nodded. 'Even though I know she's still in the picture.'

Pete shrugged. 'I've tried to be discreet.'

'I know you have, but I can read you like a comic.

139

Anyway, I think Kathy's good for you. She's a sensible girl, from what I know of her. A practical person. You need somebody like that to shove you now an' then.'

'Mum's convinced she's no better than a streetwalker.'

'Mum'll change her mind. One day.'

Pete didn't look convinced of that, but he nodded anyway. 'So what have you got to tell me?'

'It's a long story, but I'll shorten it as much as I can. It all started when I found out I'd got a dicky heart.'

Pete stared at him.

'It's not serious enough to kill me or put me in a wheelchair. In fact it's not serious at all. But I've got to take things easier. I've known it for quite a long time, an' I've been makin' arrangements. They've taken a long time, too.'

Pete was still staring. 'Does Mum know about your heart?'

'No. An' I don't want her told, Pete. She'd only start frettin' an' findin' ways to blame herself.'

'An' you're sure it's nothin' too serious?'

'Positive. Dr Legg told me himself. I just have to make a few changes, an' I'll live as long as Methuselah.'

Pete nodded, reassured. If Dr Legg said it was so, then it was so. 'What are these arrangements you've made?'

'Me an' Gail's movin' out to Romford. I've got a new job. I'll be managin' a fruit an' veg shop. No more heavin' an humpin' an' standin' about in the cold.'

'Good God.' Pete shook his head, considering the implications. 'That's one thing you'll not keep from Mum. She'll go spare. She always gets dead shaky when any of us talks about movin' away.'

'I'll take care of it all,' Ronnie said. 'I'll point out there's a spare room in our new house. It'll be somewhere she can come an' stop on the odd weekend.' He looked squarely at Pete. 'That brings us to your bonus. You've done well by yourself, like we hoped you would. You've a job, a place to live, a chance to grab yourself a decent future. So, I'm lettin' you have the stall.'

Pete looked at his brother, then at his drink, then across at the window. 'Bloody hell, Ron . . .' He swallowed the rest of the brandy and sat panting softly as the fumes spread. 'This has been quite a day.'

'I'm not givin' you the business for nothin', mind. We'll agree a price, then we'll agree a down-payment an' a fair monthly instalment.'

'Instalments,' Pete said, grinning. 'It's like bein' back in court.' He shook his head in bewilderment. 'Christ, I don't know what to say.'

'You like the idea?'

'I love the idea. I've envied you that stall for years. When you finally bought it off Mum I thought to meself, that's that. Ron's tuckin' it under his arm for keeps.' Slowly, he rubbed his fingertips on his forehead. 'I'll need time to take this in.'

'Have another drink while you're doin' it.'

As Ronnie drained his glass and went to the bar, Pete sank back in the seat, trying to encompass his luck. It was incredible. His future was laid on. In one day he had been granted the lot. He was a free man. He would soon have a decent income, the privilege of making decisions, an opportunity to expand. Everything, in fact, he had ever wanted. Or almost everything. The rest would be attended to in short order.

When Ronnie brought the fresh drinks Pete thanked him again, toasted his future and Gail's with the brandy, then swallowed it in two gulps.

'You'll get pissed at that rate,' Ronnie warned him.

'That's my last drink today,' Pete promised. 'What I'm goin' to do now is sit here while you have your beer, an' I'm goin' to ask you a zillion questions about the business. Then, when it's time for you to go back to the stall, I'm goin' to get on the blower an' tell Kathy.'

'You won't need to ask me many questions, Pete.

Gail's written it all out for you. The official handbook of Beale's Fruit 'n' Veg.'

The brandy warmed Pete's sudden billowing of emotion. 'I'll never be able to thank you enough,' he murmured. He reached out and squeezed Ronnie's arm. 'I'll not let you down. Bank on that.'

'You'd better not. If you do, I'll wallop you.'

Pete smiled. 'I'll tell you somethin' about that ticker of yours.'

'What?'

'Dodgy or not, it's one of the biggest I've ever come across.'

15

Arthur turned the page of his newspaper and folded it flat. The crackle annoyed Louise, who was sitting on the couch with wool and needles poised, trying to concentrate on the knitting pattern beside her. She glared at him over the top of her glasses. Arthur, oblivious, frowned with concentration as his eye ran down the column of print.

'Stone the crows,' he said.

Louise glared at him again.

'Whatever next?' he murmured, grinning at the paper.

'Did you say somethin'?' Louise snapped.

Arthur looked up. 'What?'

'I asked if you'd said somethin'. You was definitely mumblin'.'

'I was just readin' this.'

'Out loud? Do you have to read out loud?'

'I wasn't readin' it out loud at all . . .'

'Well, you was makin' some sort of noise. Gruntin' and mumblin'.'

'If I was, I didn't know I was doin' it.'

'Well you was doin' it, all right. An' very aggravatin' it can be, I might tell you.'

Pauline came down the stairs, yawning. It was the third week of the ninth month of her pregnancy. Each afternoon she went to bed for an hour. She glanced warily at her mother as she crossed the room. Louise was still staring accusingly at Arthur.

'What's up, Mum?'

'Nothin's up.' Louise put down her knitting. 'You sit here, I'll go an' make us a cup of tea.' She threw a hard look at Arthur as she went through to the kitchen.

Pauline sat down on the couch. Arthur looked across at her and smiled.

'Had a nice little kip?'

'Yeah.' Pauline yawned again. 'I don't know as all this sleepin' does me much good, mind you. It seems to make me a lot more tired.'

'You know what Dr Legg said. You're a bit anaemic so you've got to rest up when you can.'

Pauline sighed. 'I'll be glad when I've had this baby. It seems to have been on the way forever.'

Arthur's attention had already gone back to the newspaper. He read in silence for a minute as Pauline sat thoughtfully rubbing her stomach.

'You'll never believe this,' Arthur said, without taking his eyes from the paper. 'That Kenneth Tynan – you know, the one that did the effin' an' blindin' on television a while back – he's puttin' on a show up West where all the actors and actresses are naked the whole time.'

'Smut,' Pauline said without emphasis. 'He'll get away with callin' it art, of course.'

'Yeah, likely.' Arthur read on, quoting another couple of snippets of show-business news as he went. Cilla Black had married Bobby Willis, her road manager. The forthcoming Rolling Stones' concert in Hyde Park was predicted to be one of the biggest events of its kind ever staged.

'I don't like them Rollin' Stones,' Pauline said. They were too harsh for her. Too threatening. She preferred the Beatles, if she had to make the choice. At least they had some good tunes, and Paul McCartney had a really cute little baby face. Mick Jagger, on the other hand, looked horrible. The whole group looked horrible. 'I reckon they're encouragin' it, the whole drugs an' sex thing that's sweepin' the country. What they do, the kids do.' Pauline drew solace from the performers who obviously lived by decent standards. People like Val Doonican.

Louise's voice broke the air, shrill and petulant. 'How many times have I asked? How many times? I might as well talk to the bloody wall!'

Arthur and Pauline looked at each other. For over a month, since Ronnie had finally told his mother he was moving to Romford, Louise had been more querulous and irritable than usual. Much more.

'What is it now, Mum?' Pauline called.

'This sugar jar! It's a disgrace!' She appeared in the doorway holding the offending container. 'Look at it! Just look! Bits of coffee all mixed through the sugar! It's disgustin'!' The jar was being shown to Pauline, but Louise's eyes were on Arthur.

'My fault,' Arthur muttered. 'Sorry.'

'Sorry isn't good enough,' Louise grumbled, turning away again. 'I didn't spend all these years keepin' my house an' my things clean an' decent, just so's somebody that don't know any better can come in an' turn the place into a pigsty.'

Arthur glared after her. 'Now hang on a minute . . .'

'Arthur,' Pauline hissed. 'Leave it. She's just on edge.'

'She's got no right slangin' me just because she's feelin' rough. No right at all.'

He got up and went through to the kitchen. Louise turned from the work top and scowled at him.

'I'd be obliged if you'd keep your remarks about me to yourself,' Arthur told her. 'I've had it to the neck with you complainin' about how I do things wrong. I'd take it as a kindness if you'd pack it in, all right?'

'Don't you talk to me like that in me own house!'

'Well come outside an' I'll do it there.'

In the front room Pauline groaned and rolled her eyes towards the ceiling. Her mother's endless moaning had begun to work a change in Arthur. Most of the time he was still his complacent, easygoing self, but two or three times lately he had really lost his temper. In all the time Pauline had known him, she had never seen that happen

145

before. The trouble was, when he got ratty the old lady got worse.

Louise appeared by the side of the couch, flushed and breathing hard. 'I'm not havin' him talkin' to me like that,' she informed Pauline.

'Oh Mum. Calm down. You're makin' a lot of fuss about nothin'.'

'Nothin'? So that's what he's doin', is it? Turnin' the place into a doss house is nothin', is it?'

'Mum!'

'You brought him into my home. You see to it he behaves right.'

It was time, Pauline decided, to bring this turbulence to a head. She stood up as Arthur came back into the room. '*You* invited us to stay here,' she told her mother, folding her arms and duplicating Louise's domineering stance. 'We didn't force ourselves on you. If you think it was a mistake havin' us here just say so an' we'll sod off some place else.'

'Huh.' Louise's eyes betrayed a sudden uncertainty. 'Where could you go, then? Tell me that.'

'Anywhere. Anywhere at all to get away from your constant bitchin'.'

'What kind of way is that to talk to me? You're no better than he is.'

Pauline took a deep breath, showing Louise the determined set of her jaw. 'Listen to me Mum. We'll push off if you want us to. We might just to it anyway. I've had enough an' Arthur's had plenty.'

'What's he had to put up with, compared to me?' Louise demanded.

'You're never off his top. Every night when he comes home there's somethin' up. You draw complaints out of thin air. You're even worse at weekends. Look at today. Saturday's supposed to be a day off for him – some bloody day off with you nigglin' an' bawlin' all the time!'

'Stop exaggeratin' . . .'

146

'I'm not. You was grumblin' when I went up to bed an' you'd a face like a fizz when I came back down. It's been non-stop.'

'That's not fair,' Louise whined. This confrontation didn't suit her. Pauline had too much ammunition. She had even defused Louise's major weapon, the threat of eviction, before she had thought of using it. 'I only make a fuss when it's called for.'

'You do it because you're upset at Ronnie movin' away. You have to take your hurt out on somebody, so Arthur keeps catchin' it. Well, we're not standin' for any more.'

In the circumstances, Louise saw only one thing to do before this confrontation got completely beyond her control.

'I'm goin' to me bedroom!' She turned and stamped off up the stairs.

Arthur waited until he heard the bedroom door close, then he said, 'Did you mean that? About leavin'?'

'Well.' Pauline shrugged. 'It wasn't all bluff. If she got me mad enough, I would walk out. Wouldn't you?'

'I suppose so.' Now that he thought about it, he had probably been angry enough with Louise, a time or two lately, to do just that. Where he would go to after he was out – well, that was a mystery to him.

'We'd get by,' Pauline said.

Arthur had just tried to picture it happening. 'She'd never let you go,' he said. 'Not in your condition.'

'I know.' Pauline gave him an almost mischievous little smile. 'Look, let's just you an' me sit down an' have a bit of peace on our own while we can, eh?'

Up in her room Louise sat down by the window, dabbing away a few salt tears that had sprung forward as she shut the door. 'Silly old duffer,' she rebuked herself.

During the war when she had been just a little older than Pauline was now, Louise had taught herself to stay well clear of self-pity. It had been a survival tactic, a necessary one to combat fear and uncertainty. She'd had to face interminable days without knowing if her husband was alive or dead. If she had felt sorry for herself in those circumstances, there was no saying what might have happened to her.

And yet, after learning that powerful lesson all those years ago, here she was, feeling put-upon, ill done-by, shuffling about the place all day wearing her poor-me face.

She knew what the big difference was, of course. There was no Albert any more. At one time there had been her twin concerns, Albert and the kids. Now it was just the kids. They were everything. And that central preoccupation of her life was being whittled and diminished in a way that hurt Louise to her soul.

She thought sourly about Dora and decided not to feel surprised if she never saw her again. Pete, one day, might turn out to be the kind of lad she wanted him to be, but for the present she couldn't feel easy about his future. As for Harry, she didn't know what was going on in his life. There was still no sign of him settling down, and the last time she saw him he had been drinking seriously again. Kenny, who should have grown up long ago and settled down, still behaved like a teenager. She hardly ever saw him; he was always out with his mates, having his fun, putting off a man's life and its responsibilities.

And now Ronnie was going away. That was one of the hardest blows she had ever had to suffer. Ronnie, the shy one, who for six days a week, over the last thirteen years, had been just beyond her back yard gate carrying on the family business from the same stall Albert had used. It was terrible to think he wouldn't be there any more. Knowing Pete would be there in his place was some consolation, but she would rather the exchange didn't take place. The sense of something precious coming to an end was painfully dispiriting.

Louise had to admit it; Pauline was her only solace.

She had her there, in her own home, on the point, almost, of presenting her with a grandchild. In her self-pitying distress, she would have to be careful not to bring another ending on herself, another grievous parting.

Pauline and Arthur were sitting side by side on the couch when Louise came back downstairs. They didn't turn to look at her, but she saw their stiffness, their alertness to her presence.

Louise went towards the kitchen. 'Just you two hang on a minute,' she said gently as she went past. 'I'll get us that cup of tea.'

The little flat offered up its modest, tidy welcome as Pete and Kathy came into the living room and stood looking around them. The night before, Pete had spent two hours washing down paintwork, hoovering, dusting and polishing. He had even put flowers in the vase on the coffee table.

'You've got it looking smashin', Pete.' Kathy kissed his cheek. 'I'll see it stays this way.'

'You'll have to. I'll be too knackered to do more than collapse on the settee, after floggin' me wares all day.'

'You've a couple of weeks yet before you start that.' She sighed contentedly. 'Two weeks to ourselves. Luxury.'

'No sneakin' in an' out any more, either.'

Kathy grinned. 'I'll have a job keepin' meself from tiptoein' for the first day or two,' she warned him. 'Gettin' used to bein' legal won't just happen overnight.'

The raw sensations, the residue of the past few difficult days, had dropped away as soon as they entered the Registrar's room. Less than an hour before, with no members of their families present, nor any friends, they had become man and wife. The fact was witnessed by two of the Registrar's assistants.

'The flat feels different already,' Kathy said. 'Now that it's home.'

'Yeah, it does.' Pete ran his hand along the back of a chair. 'We can be in it now without wonderin' if I'll end the night gettin' a hammerin', or if you'll be goin' back to a bit of domestic hell.'

It all came back to Kathy like the unwelcome, unasked-for abridgement of a bad dream. There had been so many threats, humiliations, even physical punishments. At the last, there had been heated arguments, then her cold statement to her family, an announcement both of their failure to break her and of her personal victory. She was going to marry Pete Beale, she told them, and no one would stop her.

Her father's sneering, mean-spirited response had been predictable; 'Go to him then, you little slut. He's welcome to you. Neither one of you's gettin' a bargain.' Her mother had chosen tight-lipped silence. Her brothers, allowing Colin to be the spokesman of their unanimous response to her news, expressed scant interest – after all, Colin pointed out, she was no part of that family any more.

'I'll go an' tell Mum tomorrow,' Pete said.

Kathy reached for his hand and clasped it. 'Come over here.' She led him to the settee. They sat down. Still holding his hand, Kathy looked steadily into Pete's eyes and said, 'Whatever your Mum believes, or what anybody else just says for spite, I'm goin' to be a good wife to you. The best you could have.'

'I know that.'

'Hear it, anyway.' Her face was serious, her eyes bright and determined. 'You were the biggest thing in my future before you even knew it. I'll not forget how lucky I've been – it's not everybody's dreams that come true.'

'Yeah, well . . .' Pete drew her close. 'I've been a lot luckier than you.'

Kathy wrinkled her nose. 'We'll have a bull an' cow about that after. The thing I most want to say, Pete, is

I'll live up to you. An' I'll make sure you turn out to be everythin' you can be.'

Pete looked down at their joined hands and shook his head. 'I'm still not sure it's happened, you know. I feel . . .' He thought for a moment. 'I feel like it would maybe be a good thing if I'd broke me leg. It's like I haven't done enough to deserve all that's happened.'

Kathy released his hand and slid her arm around his waist. 'The way I'm goin' to push you, Sunshine,' she said, 'you'll soon feel like you've earned the lot.'

16

Memories flooded. Louise saw her mother, clear as day, and her grandmother, dear lost faces smiling at her down the tunnel of time. She remembered a sunlit field – a Sunday school outing, at Chingford Mount. All the girls were in snow white pinafores and button boots, decorating the horse-drawn brake with paper streamers and huge bunches of asters. She could smell the heat under the big tent as they sat row on row, drinking hot tea, eating brown bread with butter and jam. Friends, so many of them gone, called to her from a time of hot dusty pavements, tin Cocoa adverts on shop fronts, boys in patched trousers, clear fruit gums, Friday-night baths in front of the fire.

Louise turned away from the window and wondered vaguely if she should have another cup of tea. She often wondered how much tea she had drank in her fifty-four years. It was her refresher, time-filler, comforter – and she did need some now, she decided, making for the kitchen.

Together or separately, tea and memory were powerful consolers. The memories came to her often these days, usually when she was lonely, or annoyed, or hurt to a point where she needed the soothing retreat of the past and its simplicity.

As Louise filled the kettle, she reminded herself that it hadn't been all that simple or especially soothing in those days. It had been downright nasty a lot of the time. She could recall, as clearly as the nice times, the awful occasions when her head was searched for lice, the doses of castor oil, the discomfort of ill-fitting shoes and itchy school clothes. It was easy to call back the smell of horse dung wafting through her mother's house, foul-belching drains and the droning hordes of flies in summer. There were memories of grim schoolteachers who wielded rulers that rapped knuckles whenever a word was misread or a scratchy nib made a blot. Her childhood had been populated by old people with terrible breath, rude boys and rough ones who said and did shocking things, roaring drunk men and a succession of fiercely religious neighbours and aunts.

'Even so,' Louise murmured. Childhood memories were still a great comfort. They made her remember what it was like to have the whole of life in front of her, and helped her forget the heartaches of the moment. Today, they had diverted her from the shock of Pete's news, from the hurt of what he had done and what she had said to him.

Pauline came into the kitchen. She was very pale and her eyes had a glassy, feverish cast.

'You all right, girl?'

'I've felt better.'

'You shouldn't be standin'.' Louise leaned forward and examined her face closely. 'Your lips are all chalky. You look as if you've had a shock.'

'I'm not surprised, the way you went on at our Pete.'

'Oh.' Louise looked away, fussing with the teapot. 'You was listenin', then.'

'I couldn't help it, could I? The sound travels up through them floorboards like they wasn't there – especially when somebody's bawlin' an' shoutin'.'

'It'd make a bloody saint shout,' Louise said. 'Imagine. Sneakin' off an' marryin' that connivin' slut . . .'

'She ain't a slut,' Pauline told her sharply. 'I've known Kathy Hills since she was a kid. She's quite nice when you get to know her.'

'Nice? Nice girls don't carry on with married men, do they? An' decent blokes don't abandon their kids an' run around with the likes of her, come to that.'

153

'That's not fair, Mum. You shouldn't go judgin' Kathy that way when you won't take the trouble to know her properly.' Pauline drew her cardigan about her and folded her arms. 'You just make heartache for yourself, bein' so stubborn.'

'I've got me own standards an' me own point of view.'

'So had Hitler.'

'Now look here, Pauline – '

Pauline groaned. 'I don't want to talk about it. I'm goin' to sit down.' She spread her hands on either side of her abdomen. 'I'm sure this tyke's on the move, you know.'

Louise stiffened. 'What do you mean?'

'Well, it feels a lot lower, an' heavier . . .'

'Go an' sit down this minute,' Louise ordered. 'Put your feet up. On you go.'

Pauline shuffled through to the front room and lowered herself on to the couch. She lay back on the cushions at one end and swung her legs up, letting her heels settle on another cushion.

Poor old Pete, she thought. His mum had really let rip. She had told him, finally, to get out of her house. Over the years, they had all come to learn what that meant; if Louise told anyone to get out, they had to stay out until they were invited back. There was, though, the consolation of knowing that whether Mum believed it or not, Pete had landed on his feet. Kathy would look after him, Pauline had no doubts on that score.

'Where's Arthur?' Louise called from the kitchen.

'Over at the Vic. I told him to go an' have a pint before his dinner. He's been makin' me nervous, askin' every five minutes if I'm all right.'

Louise came to the doorway. 'You can't blame him. It's quite a worryin' time for a man too, you know. I remember what your dad was like . . .'

'Yeah,' Pauline sighed. 'I suppose it can be a bit of a strain.'

'Oh it can, believe me.'

Louise turned back to the kitchen as another skein of memory unfolded. She saw Albert, round-eyed with wonderment as he held their firstborn. She blinked back a tear and lifted the boiling kettle off the gas.

In the Queen Victoria Harold Legg was rounding off the morning with a half pint of bitter. Ethel Skinner was beside him at the bar, unreeling a string of gossip to Polly, the landlady.

Harold had decided, two weeks ago, that the surgery was the best place for the framed pictures of Israel his mother kept sending. He didn't really want them at home. That morning he had nailed them up on the blank expanses of wall on either side of his desk. He had also sorted out his filing system and filled in some overdue forms for the NHS. Now he believed he could face Monday-morning surgery without the disheartening feeling that things were piling up.

Ethel turned to him as Polly moved away to serve a customer. 'I thought you was goin' to your friend's for the weekend,' she said. She rarely forgot the highlights of the doctor's social diary, which she assiduously winkled from him at every opportunity.

'I was, but then I changed my mind. Too much to do here.' He smiled. 'Besides, I suspect my friend had plans to introduce me to another eligible lady or two.'

'You should've gone, then. The company of ladies is good for a man in your position, if you don't mind me sayin' so.' She sniffed. 'A lot better than hangin' about in a pub. You're tempted to stay, if there's nobody waitin' for you at home, or someplace else.'

'I'm not hanging about, Ethel. I'm having one drink, then I'm leaving.'

'It can lead to that, though.'

Harold frowned at her. 'What can lead to what?'

Ethel pursed her bright lips for a moment, the way an

155

expert would before issuing a learned opinion. 'Livin' on your own, especially when you're a man still in his prime – it can lead to hangin' about places like this, surroundin' yourself with boozers. Look at Reg Cox. On his own at home all these years. So what does he do? Sits in the corner there swillin' beer every hour they're open – I reckon he lives on nothin' but bitter an' crisps.'

Harold glanced at Reg, who was trying to crush and damp-down a whole mouthful of potato crisps before they choked him.

'It's no way to live,' Ethel muttered.

Harold nodded. 'The drunkard and the glutton shall come to poverty,' he intoned, 'and drowsiness shall clothe a man with rags.'

'Sorry?' Ethel looked faintly alarmed.

'It's from my mother's favourite guide to living, Ethel. The Old Testament.'

'Oh.' Her eyes betrayed a sudden anxiety to change the subject. 'Did you hear about young Den Watts an' that Angie Shaw?'

Harold thought for a moment. He knew Angie all right. She had visited him in the surgery quite a few times and he remembered lecturing her, several years before, on the foolishness of regarding the Pill as a passport to unbridled, indiscriminate sex. He wasn't sure he knew Den, though.

'What about them?' he asked.

'They've run off an' got married. Imagine.'

'I thought you were in favour of marriage.'

'Of course I am, Doctor, when the couple know what they're doin'. But them two – well. They ain't *half* mature enough yet. I can't imagine them settlin' down to just each other's company. Not for long, anyway.'

'Perhaps they'll surprise you.'

Ethel snorted as she picked up her glass. 'I'm sure they'll do that all right. One way or another.'

Arthur Fowler came to the bar to have his glass refilled. He had The News of the World folded under his arm.

'Mornin', Doctor. Ethel.'

Harold nodded. 'What's in the paper today, Arthur? Anything exciting?'

'Nah.' Arthur slid his glass across to Polly. 'The scandal rags ain't what they used to be.' He grinned. 'In the old days, when they reported stories about eighty-year-old bishops an' chorus girls, or vergers an' choirboys – '

'Or doctors an' patients,' Ethel cut in with a wicked chuckle.

'Yeah, whatever,' Arthur grunted. 'Anyway, when they reported cases like that, they always used to say "an incident took place". Nowadays they tell you what happened, straight out. There's no room for imagination any more.'

'If you ask me,' Ethel chimed in again, 'people's morals has gone down the drain. I mean, look at that Christine Keeler business.'

'That was a while ago, Ethel,' Arthur said.

'I know it was. But it just shows you the state the modern world's in.' She had a faraway look for a moment. 'Mind you, it wasn't all keepin' your hand on your ha'penny in my young day, either. There was quite a few flashy, loose-livin' women round the part of Camden Town where I grew up.'

Polly put Arthur's drink on the bar. 'I remember the type,' she said. 'Fur coats an' no knickers.'

As Ethel went into a small chuckling fit Harold decided he would stay for another drink. There were times when the random, rootless talk in the bar provided the perfect antidote to a week's payload of vexation and worry.

'Another half for me please, Polly,' he said, knowing there was a risk of Ethel telling him he *did* have a tendency to hang around the pub. 'Let me get yours, Arthur,' he added. 'And another one for Ethel, please.'

Since the days of Harold's childhood in the East End,

he had relished the people's humour and the flexibility of their conversation. Nothing much was ever learned from listening to them, none of life's mysteries came anywhere near to being clarified, let alone solved. But that was hardly the point. These people embraced life without needing to analyze it or wanting to take it very seriously. The few serious exchanges he had heard in the Queen Victoria had not lasted. They had all been sabotaged by laughter.

Harold had taken one sip from his fresh drink when the door burst open and Louise rushed in.

'Arthur,' she panted, 'you'll have to get the – ' She stopped when she saw Harold. 'Doctor. Can you come? It's Pauline. The baby's started.'

He put down the glass and went quickly to the door with Arthur behind him.

'I'll just get my bag from the car, Lou. You go back to the house and keep an eye on her. I'll be there in two minutes.'

As they rushed out Ethel turned and beamed at Polly. 'It's goin' to be a boy,' she said, then finished her drink in four loud gulps. 'I saw it in the leaves.' She snatched up her bag and hurried to the door. 'I'll go across an' see what I can do to help.'

When they reached the house Louise and Arthur helped Pauline upstairs to the bedroom.

'Right,' Louise grunted as they got her on to the bed. 'You go back downstairs an' get the kettle on, Arthur. I'll see to her now.'

Arthur stood by the bed, looking at Pauline, wincing with her as the spasms quickened.

'Go on,' Louise urged him. 'You can't do no good up here.' There was a growing fashion, she had heard, for men to be present at the birth of their children. She'd never heard of anything so ridiculous. If there was ever a time when a woman didn't want her husband around, this

158

was it. 'Make the tea nice an' strong. It's better for your nerves that way.'

Arthur bent down and kissed Pauline on the forehead. 'See you in a bit, love.'

On the stairs he met the doctor coming up. As they squeezed past each other Harold slapped his shoulder. 'Good job I was here, Arthur. I'd have hated to miss Pauline's first.'

First and last, Arthur thought. He didn't fancy the idea of Pauline going through all this again. Nor him, for that matter.

He waited in the kitchen for twenty minutes, consuming two cups of tea and only half hearing Ethel's commentary on what she imagined was taking place upstairs.

'He'll be a perfect baby,' she told him as he drained the second cup. 'Mark my words. Pauline won't have no trouble. No trouble at all. I know about these things.'

'Yeah?'

'Oh yes. I can tell when things is goin' right an' when they're not. It's just a gift. Everythin's fine, Arthur. One time, I was – '

Upstairs, a baby gave one sharp cry, then another. Petrified, Arthur stared at Ethel. Everything went silent. Then the crying came again, an energetic, full-throated yell.

'Now then, Dad . . .'

Arthur turned. Louise was standing in the doorway, red-eyed, smiling. 'If you give it a minute,' she said, 'you can go up an' say hello to your son.'

Arthur wanted to speak, to express his sudden, over-whelming joy. When he opened his mouth his throat tightened and sharp tears pricked his eyes. He put out his arms and closed them around Louise, hugging her.

'Well done, the pair of you,' she whispered.

As Arthur stepped back Ethel stood on her toes and kissed his cheek. 'How does it feel then?'

Arthur gazed at the window for a moment, trying to

steady his breathing. 'It feels . . .' He had to take another sharp breath. 'It feels great, Ethel. Fabulous.' He turned to Louise. 'Can I go up now?'

'Yeah, why not. Knock on the door first.'

Ethel stepped forward and gave her old friend a squeeze. Louise fumbled for her handkerchief. Memory blossomed bright again, mingling the happiness of past and present, misting her eyes and making her heart swell.